B2B
WITHOUT THE
BS

The Business-to-Business Sales & Marketing Manual

By
Robert Bell and Louis Zacharilla

Published by
Alan/Anthony, Inc.
B2B CUSTOMER CREATION

www.alananthony.com

First edition, published by Alan/Anthony, Inc., 55 Broad Street, 14th Floor, New York, NY 10004 USA – 212-825-1582 - www.alananthony.com

 Because its purpose is to create a customer, the business enterprise has two — and only these two — basic functions: marketing and innovation. Marketing and innovation alone produce results; all the rest are "costs."

— Peter Drucker, *Management,* 1973.

Contents

Why Aren't My People Selling More?

The complaint is probably as old as human commerce. And it is just as painful today, in the Digital Age, as it probably was back in the Bronze Age.

Here in the Digital Age, though, you'll find lots of companies with a diagnosis. Your problem is that your Web site isn't enabled for e-commerce, or that you don't have a Customer Relationship Management system, or that your salespeople don't have the product catalog on their Palm Pilots. And they just happen to have the e-commerce software, the CRM platform or the sales force management system to solve it.

The truth is more mundane — but a lot more useful. There are three, and only three, possible reasons why people selling services or products to business customers (B2B) aren't selling more.

■ **They don't know how.** That is, they may be good intuitive salespeople who have a sufficient understanding of your products and services. But they lack the professional skills to consistently perform up to their potential. Or maybe they are engineers or project managers by trade, for whom selling is a necessary evil. They know your products, services and processes inside and out, but they don't know how to apply the same discipline and process-based thinking to the job of bringing sales in the door.

■ **The person managing them — who may be you — doesn't know how.** In many B2B companies, possibly even the majority of them, salespeople don't report to an experienced sales and marketing professional. They report to the CEO or the COO or, God help them, the CFO. They report to the head programmer or the guy who runs the factory floor. So when they're going through a rough patch and need to alter something in their approach, they have nobody to turn to for advice.

■ **You're sending them into battle empty-handed.** Selling is one end of a communication, education and persuasion process with many other components. From various forms of promotion to brochures and hand-outs, your salespeople need quality support that removes barriers, helps them make their case and maintains contact through the long sales cycle.

There is actually a fourth possibility: that your products or services have lost their competitive edge. Every new product or service that achieves success starts out having a unique value, which is why customers buy it. But in a free market, competitors quickly respond by adding features to their own products and services. Within a predictable period of time, your innovative product or service becomes a commodity. But product and service innovation is a big enough topic to fill a book by itself. Our goal here is to share with you the basic and powerful fundamentals of B2B marketing and sales.

The Good News

The good news about these three problems is that they are highly curable. And it doesn't take a CRM platform or wireless Palm Pilots to do it. It just takes knowledge and the old-fashioned discipline to apply it.

In the 20 short chapters of this book, we will explain how successful B2B companies create customers, and how your business can create more of them at an affordable cost.

What This Book Is — and What It Is Not

If you're looking for new paradigms, you won't find them here. We won't tell you how to thrive on chaos, virtualize your business or fit a square peg into a round hole.

Marketing and sales are business processes. Marketing is the organized discipline of understanding what you're selling, to whom and for how much — and of preparing potential customers to be sold. Sales is not about glad-handing or fast-talking or pulling the wool over somebody's eyes. It is a step-by-step method for turning possible buyers into customers.

Success in sales and marketing requires knowledgeable people with the right temperament, who go through these stages in the right order, and who track their progress so that they can fix problems before they become crises.

This book lays out the stages and activities. It provides the knowledge needed to professionalize the marketing and sales process, and it explains how to track your progress, so that you can manage what you're doing.

There's one more thing this book is: the result of the 20 years we have spent helping B2B companies create customers in sectors ranging from high-tech to industrial. It is a distillation from our experience of what works and what doesn't, what's necessary to growth and what you can honestly do without.

The Biggest Mistake

So, let's get started — with one very important question.

What's the biggest mistake people make when they approach the task of B2B selling?

The answer? They focus on the end of the process — the proposal, the negotiations and the close — instead of on the beginning. And why not? The end is the fun part. It's where the money comes in. But the beginning is where you can achieve leverage. The power of the choices you make at the beginning is multiplied by the talents of your people and the network of relationships they build in the market. Like the fluttering of the butterfly's wings that supposedly leads to hurricanes in the Atlantic, those early-stage decisions and actions are what make possible the tangible successes at the end. So we're going to spend the next few chapters focusing on the beginning of the process, where doing things right can set your marketing and sales efforts on the path to amazing achievement.

The Second-Biggest Mistake

Our candidate for the second-biggest mistake is lack of continuity. Whatever sales and marketing decisions you make need to be sustainable. That is, you shouldn't spend so much that your first act in a downturn must be to slash spending. It never fails to amaze us how, when sales are flat or declining, companies decide to cut their sales and marketing budgets. "Hey, we have a revenue problem! Let's cut spending on the stuff that brings in revenue!"

Great idea, right?

On the other hand, you shouldn't spend so little that you fail to move the dial. That's like having a roaring headache and taking ½ of a Tylenol. Many B2B companies do this, and end up complaining that this marketing stuff is a bunch of bull. So is Tylenol if you just nibble one corner off a tablet.

A good rule of thumb is to spend enough to make yourself slightly uncomfortable, and then to grit your teeth and keep spending it when you hit a downturn. If you're a person of exceptional fortitude and have the cash in the bank, you can even *increase* your spending in a downturn. It's a great time to grab market share. In bad times, everybody is rethinking their current way of doing things and is more open than usual to vendors with new solutions. But whatever you do, avoid the mistake of cutting off the communication just as the battle for customers gets fierce.

B2B
Marketing
Strategy

What's the Value?

Value in Flux

Ready! Fire! Aim!

Targeting Essentials

Price Pointers

CHAPTER 1

What's the Value?

Captain Ahab had his undying obsession: the Great White Whale. For most people who sell products or services B2B, the really big fish is *price*.

Every marketing executive who has ever had a slow quarter knows that a price cut is the answer. Every big deal, where the competition gets hot, has salespeople begging for a little leeway on margins. Believe it or not, we once knew a salesman whose moral compass told him that his company should only make so much money on a deal and who would cut his prices to bring it in at or below the magic number.

What most people forget is that price, by itself, is meaningless. When you find yourself obsessing about price, what you should really be worrying about is *value*.

Price has meaning only in relation to value. If customers balk at our price, it is because the value we deliver does not justify the price for that particular set of customers. We may think we are selling a premium-quality service or product, but the potential buyer may see it as a commodity. Which makes our premium-quality price look outrageous. But a potential customer who shares our view of the premium quality will find the price reasonable.

Understanding this transforms the marketing and sales process. In the universe of possible buyers there should be a group that values what we do, because it contributes to an area of vital importance in their operations. Marketing isn't about coming up with the next clever gimmick — it focuses on adding value to products and services, and communicating that value to the right audience. Selling isn't about talking fast — it's about locating prospects who value our products or services enough to pay our price, and turning them into customers. So the first place to look when faced with a marketing and sales challenge is not the price — it is the *value*.

To illustrate this principle, we'll provide some examples drawn from work with companies serving specific B2B niches, and show how the question of value provides the foundation for meeting a marketing and sales challenge.

Example: IT Services

We advised a privately held company that was a pioneer in a business we had never heard of before. Big companies with million of customers and a national network of offices face big information technology problems. Our client helped these companies with one specific aspect of the IT challenge: processing, printing and distributing millions of bills each month, or hundreds of thousands of sales reports or warrantee statements or any of the thousands of pieces of computer-generated paperwork containing data that varies from document to document. If it doesn't sound glamorous — it's not. But it is mission-critical for each customer. It offers monthly, if not daily, opportunities to screw up in a very public way. And managing this function drives many IT managers out of their minds.

The company's problem was stagnation in revenue growth. It had a very aggressive sales force, lead by an experienced professional, which had helped the company grow to about $16 million in annual sales. This made them large enough to start attracting more serious competitive attention, and they were finding deals harder to come by. They were also suffering growing pains that were causing too high a rate of customer losses.

Example: Broadband Telecommunications

Another client was in an industry *you* have probably never heard of. It was a teleport serving a metropolitan area with a heavy concentration of electronic media. A teleport is a communications hub for high-bandwidth (broadband) communications. This particular company ran a complex of over 30 satellite antennas, linked to a metro-area fiber and microwave network, and connecting with long-haul fiber circuits reaching across the country. If one of the news bureaus, TV stations or cable channels in the metro area needed to put programming up on a satellite, or send it by fiber to a customer in Los Angeles, our client's teleport was the place to go.

As with the IT company, the teleport had grown rapidly for several years under a new chief executive, but the rate of growth had suddenly stagnated. Contract renewals weren't the problem — the problem was that new business was increasingly hard to come by. This was a particular challenge because the company had recently invested several million dollars in upgrading its core facilities to handle new growth — and the prospect of payback on that investment had suddenly grown dim.

Back to Basics

With each company, our first move was to go back to basics — to revisit their understanding of the value delivered to customers, and to find out if the company's understanding was still in touch with reality. We helped the client to take a hard look at the question, "what business are we in?" and then to ask an even tougher one: "what business should we be in?"

The IT services company had a clear core value proposition. Their prospective customers were IT departments in pain: companies with severe problems in their in-house operation for printing and distributing computer-generated paperwork, or with an outside vendor who was screwing up badly. Their value, which we determined by interviewing their customers, was to process every customer invoice or recall notice or sales report on time, without errors and at minimum cost — which is to say, to do it better, faster and cheaper than it could be done in-house.

According to our interviews, this core value appeared to have as much validity today as it did when the company was founded. Yet it did not appear to be delivering the same results in terms of revenue growth as it had been. Why?

The teleport offered its customers the time and cost advantages of sharing a large and robust communications infrastructure. In essence, customers used the services of the teleport as a substitute for building their own specialized facilities. With many companies sharing the same basic infrastructure and personnel, the cost per company was lower, which created a profit margin for the teleport operator while still being cost-effective.

From customer interviews, it emerged that there was another value at work. Over the years, the teleport had built or leased fiber-optic and microwave connections to nearly every media outlet in the metro area, from sports stadiums to news bureaus, TV stations to video production companies. This had the effect of turning the teleport into a funnel for media content produced anywhere in its service area. The existence of the network made it very fast and convenient for customers to deliver TV or radio content where it needed to go, which was particularly important for breaking news. Though it wasn't a classic "outsourcer," this company's motto was "better, faster, cheaper" as well.

But new customers were suddenly hard to find. Sales growth was stalled. Why?

CHAPTER 2

Value in Flux

Value is not a static thing. A company initially succeeds because it finds a way to deliver value to customers. And it would be so much easier if the company could just go on delivering the same value to more and more customers, growing steadily bigger until it achieved a listing on the Big Board and the founders could retire filthy rich.

But in the real world, everything about the process of value delivery is in flux. The needs and desires of customers change — ironically, at least in part in response to the value they have received from your company — and partly due to factors outside your control. As a result, your product or service offerings have to change, or you have to adjust your sights to encompass new customer groups, in order to remain competitive.

Challenge for the IT Outsourcer

That was one of the challenges faced by the IT services company. Traditionally, the company sold to the vice president for information technology — a harassed individual with an ever-increasing workload, a persistently dissatisfied group of users, and a resulting high degree of paranoia. To this target group, the company sold its services based on their ability to relieve him or her of responsibility for the complex, time-consuming, error-prone and utterly un-sexy job of high-volume printing and distribution. It stressed that print-and-distribution was at the end of the IT processing chain. It could be moved outside without disrupting anything the IT department did. The company trumpeted its expertise at print processing, something that few IT departments claim as a core competency, and its state-of-the-art equipment, which few IT departments could justify buying.

The trouble was that the world had changed. First of all, this pioneering company had attracted a lot of competition, ranging from industry giants moving into its niche to start-ups pursuing the opportunity that our client had proved was there. Print-and-distribute services had increasingly become commoditized. Customers with print-and-distribute needs were receiving calls from multiple vendors, and as each competitor struggled to win, there came to be increasingly little to differentiate them except price. Our client was not, and did not try to be, the low-price vendor, but that position was under increasing threat.

To make matters worse, the print-and-distribute process was gradually expanding out from under the umbrella of the IT department. For a variety of reasons, companies gradually woke up to the fact that the customer bill or end-of-month statement was of great importance. It was often the only regular communication that companies had with their customers. It wasn't just an IT issue — it was a customer service issue and a potential competitive advantage. In the securities business, brokerages were vying to produce ever more sophisticated and user-friendly statements. In the telephone and cable TV industries, companies were struggling to introduce "bundled" billing that grouped multiple services onto a single bill.

So, while trying to deal with growing price pressure from its competition, the company was also seeing its core customer group ceding influence over the buying decision to new players that the company knew too little about. It was no wonder that growth was stagnating. The only question was whether the company would be able to adapt to the new realities in order to restart its growth engine.

Challenge for the Teleport

Market forces also affect value delivery. If your company is successful, it will inevitably attract competition. Those competitors will imitate your offerings and, in some cases, go you one better. An "arms race" develops, in which each party must strive endlessly to extend and enrich its competitive advantage in the marketplace. But unlike the nuclear arms race of the Cold War, which produced enough explosive power to destroy the world dozens of times over, commercial competitors can't afford to overbuild. Markets have saturation points where no further investment will produce results.

Our work with the teleport operator convinced us that it had become a victim of market forces. It had a fabulous network for the media market. The teleport had enjoyed such robust growth that it had stimulated competitors to set up shop in town. A couple were mom-and-pop start-ups that were more annoyance than threat. But one was the local subsidiary of a multinational communications company with a significant share of the global media market. Though it was still a fairly small presence, its brand name and global network represented significant threats.

Unfortunately, we also concluded that the market was near saturation point. This was not a scientific conclusion based on an expensive market study, but an obvious conclusion based on interviews with customers and sales people. The teleport had grown at double-digit rates by converting formerly in-house operations into new customers. These opportunities were nearly exhausted. The company's future seemed to offer two choices: resign itself to growing at the organic growth rate of the broadcast and cable industry — 5-10 percent a year — or struggle to take broadcast and cable customers from its competition.

The problem, and the solution, facing both of these companies had to do with what's called *targeting*. That's the subject of our next chapter — and we'll continue the stories there. But before we do, a word about how we developed this understanding of our clients' changing marketplace — and how you can do it for your own company.

Ask the People with the Checkbook

Marketing professionals express the distinctive value their company offers as a *value proposition*. A value proposition, like a mission statement, sums up our value in the fewest and most powerful words. Unlike most mission statements, however, it is not intended to be a substitute for action but as the foundation for action.

A value proposition answers the most challenging questions about your products or services. What do prospects find valuable about them? How does this differ from other company offerings in the same marketplace? In other words, why should they buy from you? What's in it for them?

And how do we answer these questions? The first and foremost source is one that too many companies ignore. It is the customers who already buy from you, and the prospects who give you a careful hearing — and then reject you.

The customers bought from you for a reason. They had expectations that they believed you could satisfy.

The people who rejected you originally saw enough value to give you a hearing, maybe even to request a proposal from you. But then they may have seen a mismatch between their perception of value and the price. On the other hand, they may have bought from a competitor based on political or personal considerations (like the buyer's brother-in-law who works for a competitor). Or maybe they were just tire-kicking to see what was available, or validating their current vendor's pricing, or couldn't make a decision. These latter considerations don't tell you anything — but there's a chance that talking to that prospect may reveal the dreaded price-value mismatch you need to know about.

You probably believe that you already know why customers buy from you. Maybe this is anecdotal, or perhaps you did market research some time ago. But we have found time and again that internal perceptions can vary greatly from the actual reasons that customers buy. And it is the customer's perception that counts.

Getting Down to Cases

Some of the questions we need to ask our customers and the prospects who turn us down include:

1. What were the reasons they looked at our offering originally? What were their problems or needs? Were they unhappy with their existing solution? Why?

2. What were they looking to improve? Why?

3. What value were we able to introduce? What made it more valuable than another alternative, if it was?

4. What objections or concerns did they have about our solution?

5. Who made the final decision? What were their titles, positions and departments?

6. What were their expectations after the sale?

7. Were these expectations met? If not, where did we or the competitor fall short?

8. From an overview perspective: what do they like about us? What would they like to see us improve? What would they like to see us continue doing?

9. Would they be willing to serve as a referral? Why or why not?

These can be tough questions to ask a customer. The reasons for *not* asking the questions are legion. We might irritate the customer. We might raise doubts in the customer's mind about our value. Worst of all, we might hear something we don't want to hear.

So, instead of asking, we commission market research. We do customer satisfaction surveys to see how well we are doing. We may even do something as bone-headed as the telephone company that had its customer service reps ends every call with the question, "Have I provided you with outstanding service today?" In a courtroom, that's called "leading the witness."

More Valuable Than Market Research

Our counsel is simple. Take your courage in both hands, pick a customer who likes you, and ask him or her to spend fifteen minutes helping you to better understand your own business. People like to help and are usually willing to do so. If you honestly seek their counsel, they will feel good afterward about the time spent with you.

Do this a few times. Grip your courage harder and start asking the questions of prospects whom you failed to sell.

Now, buoyed by your success, organize a Key Customer Advisory Board for your organization. Invite onto it the senior executives of your major customers, as well as of companies you would like to do business with. Start as high in the organization as you can; your request may be delegated downward, but you increase your odds of filling your Advisory Board with decision-makers. The Advisory Board will work best if it represents many different industries. You don't want, and won't get, two direct competitors sitting down next to each other.

Hold half-day or full-day meetings (depending on how much ground there is to cover) two to three times a year, and do it at a nice hotel or conference facility. The purpose of the meetings is to acquaint members with your latest activities, present investment or other decisions you are grappling with and ask advice, and to learn about your members' problems and concerns.

Why would executives of your customers agree to participate? They will be flattered, for one thing They will also be interested in making personal connections with other members of the Advisory Board. And they will probably be impressed by the fact that you care enough about their views to go to all this trouble.

One final note: you will probably want to hire a consultant to run this for you rather than trying to do it yourself. The consultant will make the invitations, develop the agendas and meeting arrangements, run the meetings, and do a post-meeting debriefing with your staff. During the meeting itself, your people should mostly keep their mouths shut and listen. It is all too easy, when faced with criticism or good advice, to respond defensively, and that will quickly destroy the effectiveness of the Advisory Board. The consultant serves as a helpful go-between and keeps the tone of the meetings friendly and professional. Most important, the consultant is viewed by both you and your Advisory Board members as a third-party without a personal ax to grind.

We guarantee that you will learn more talking to your customers and prospects — whether informally or through a formal Advisory Board — than from tens of thousands of dollars of market research. You will learn why customers buy from you, what they like and dislike about you, and how you stack up against competing offerings. This are the basic ingredients that marketers and salespeople need to change what doesn't work in your sales, marketing products, services or customer service.

CHAPTER 3

Ready! Fire! Aim!

There are over 1 billion people in China. If we start selling in China, we will only have to close one-tenth of one percent of them to be rich beyond our wildest dreams. Let's do it!

This is what passes for *targeting* in the minds of many people in business. It's the kind of thinking that our venture capitalist partners see in business plans every day — and which causes them to close the proposal and toss it away.

What's wrong with it? It's the equivalent of a hunter saying, "I know there are deer in these woods. So you start the fire and I'll be back in a few minutes with dinner." It blithely ignores the difficulties of tracking, stalking and inflicting lethal damage on a creature that survives by its stealth and speed.

An experienced hunter knows that these things take time and luck — but most of all the skill to identify signs, track the quarry and move into position for the kill.

What is Targeting?

Targeting is the methodical task of reducing the scope of your search for new customers in order to bring home the venison more often. Through the exercise of targeting, we try to set our sights on the 5-25% of the market that is likely to buy from us and ruthlessly eliminate the 75-95% who never will. The point is to increase our chances of talking to a real buyer from one in a million to something less than one in a hundred.

We used the words "ruthlessly eliminate" in the last paragraph for a reason. Most people in business instinctively dislike the idea of eliminating part of their market from consideration. They will agree intellectually that only a small proportion of the total market will actually buy from them, but when we propose to eliminate certain categories from consideration, they grow uncomfortable. They don't like the sharp lines separating worthwhile from worthless that we are trying to draw on the market map. They chafe at the idea of rules that restrict sales activity to narrow segments.

What's going on? Nothing more than human nature at work. We tend to like what we sell. We think it's neat. We think that everybody could benefit from it and put money in our pockets as a result. Even if we are infected by the germ of cynicism — like the sales team we overheard making up their own version of the company slogan: "At least we don't suck all the time" — we all need to feel that the next one could be *The One*. This is the essential force that makes state lotteries work. As the brilliant slogan of the New York State Lottery put it, "All it takes is a dollar and a dream." Whereas the real odds of winning it big are greater than the odds of being struck by an asteroid on Friday at noon.

"We Already Know Everybody"

There's a flip side to this psychology, as there is to most things human. We first ran into it in trying to convince a business owner to invest money in marketing. "We don't need it," he said. "We already know everybody in our market."

"You're right," we answered. (Always a good way to start!) "You already know everybody — that is, everybody that you already know. But what about the people you don't already know who might buy from you?"

This business owner had fallen victim to the delusion that his market was fixed: a certain group of people in a certain geographic market or industrial niche. The truth is that markets, like value, are never fixed. They grow, stagnate or shrink. Technology changes. Buyer characteristics and needs change. New competitors enter with a better idea and the funds to execute it.

Targeting for the Teleport:
The Unsophisticated Buyer

Facing suspected saturation of one market niche, we set out to find a more attractive niche for our teleport operator to serve. We began as always by making sure we understood the characteristics of existing buyers, as well as the opportunities created by the teleport's location, changes in the economic environment, and new technology.

We learned that media industry buyers are typically VPs of operations for the major networks, cable channels and news organizations. They are usually veterans of the business. They know the technology, they understand how services are delivered, and with years of experience buying a fairly static range of services and products, they know what things cost.

In other words, they are what we call sophisticated buyers.

There's a chain of discount clothing stores in the New York metropolitan area whose slogan is, "An educated consumer is our best customer." Nice slogan. But it would be closer to the truth to say, "A sophisticated buyer is our worst nightmare." Sophisticated buyers understand what you're selling (maybe better than you do) and know what things cost, so they naturally resist letting you package a solution for them. The packaging of the solution has less value to them than the savings they get by buying the pieces and assembling the solution themselves. The savings they achieve come directly from the margin you might otherwise have earned.

Unsophisticated buyers, on the other hand, will value your expertise and experience more highly. They will need you to assemble an end-to-end solution for them rather than developing it themselves from products and services they buy from you and other vendors.

Don't make the mistake of thinking that, by "sophisticated" and "unsophisticated," we mean "savvy" and "stupid." It's not the people that are different; it's the market. Sophisticated buyers are nearly always found in stable markets, like the TV and radio distribution business, where buyers can build up experience over the years in a limited field of knowledge. Unsophisticated buyers are typical of dynamic markets, where technology or business practices are subject to rapid change. In these markets, buyers have different priorities. It doesn't pay them to spend the time needed to keep up with the latest technology, process or practice. That's why they value the packaging of an end-to-end solution more than its additional cost.

So, given a choice, it's better to sell in dynamic than stable markets, and to unsophisticated than sophisticated buyers, if you're looking for growth.

Say Hello to the Internet

What our teleport client needed was a set of unsophisticated buyers, located in the same geographic area, that had developed a need for satellite services. And as so often happens, once we framed the problem clearly, we practically broke a leg stumbling over the answer.

One of the salespeople had recently unearthed a couple of opportunities involving something called the Internet. (This was back in the 1990s.) The potential customers were Internet Service Providers (ISPs) in overseas markets that needed a broadband connection to the US Internet backbone, where most of the world's Internet content resides. They operated in second and third-tier markets like Brazil and Latvia where ISPs paid huge prices to their national monopoly phone companies to get a broadband circuit to the US. These markets had also recently changed regulations to allow competition in satellite services, making it possible to connect to them via satellite. Some back-of-the-envelope calculations made it appear that the teleport could charge these ISPs half of what they were paying now and still earn handsome returns.

Voila! A new market. The buyers were data guys who knew nothing about satellite. All they knew was that they needed a circuit that could push so many kilobits or megabits of data through the pipe per second. Best of all. geography was on the teleport's side. It was located only a dozen miles from MAE East, the largest Internet network node on the East Coast. Proximity meant relatively low costs for a broadband fiber-optic connection between the teleport and the MAE.

It wasn't quite time to break out the champagne. Changing over to serve a new target market is never easy. Our teleport client was almost as ignorant about the world of ISPs as they were about satellite communications. But it found some outside consultants to advise it, and succeeded in winning an Internet via satellite contract, buying the new equipment and fiber connections it needed, and making the service work.

Having done it once, the company was ready to go to market in a more serious way. With our help, the company focused its sales and marketing resources on ISPs. It had its consultants train salespeople to understand the customer needs and technology. It exhibited at Internet trade shows overseas. It did a deal with an international systems integration firm that could install the satellite facilities its customers needed.

Within two years, the company had transformed its business from one that earned 85% of revenues from broadcasters and cable channels to one that earned 60% of revenues from Internet services. It had targeted a fast-growing market with much healthier margins that could supplement and then overtake its former core business. Even after the first great dotcom bubble burst — and caused them a lot of pain — the company still had a far healthier mix of business with much greater opportunities for growth than ever before.

CHAPTER 4

Targeting Essentials

How do you begin to apply targeting discipline to your own company? Any group of target customers can be described using five characteristics. We'll take them one by one, from the simplest and most straightforward to the most complex and subtle.

Five Characteristics

1. <u>Geography.</u> Your customers will usually be geographically close to you, often to the point of allowing you to draw circle(s) on a map with your office(s) at the center and a radius of 50 to 200 miles — whatever a reasonable driving distance may be in your area. The importance of geography depends on how important personal relationships and face-to-face meetings are in your business, how unique your offerings are, and other factors. Professional services firms and industrial testing companies, for example, typically need to be within driving distance of their clients. Travel agencies, teleport operators and many financial institutions do not. Big-ticket sales may justify a larger geographic area, whereas low-price selling does not.

2. <u>Industry.</u> Your products and services may sell to specific industries, because only those industries have a use for them. An example would be companies that make TV programs. They sell to the TV networks, cable channels and a small number of enterprise customers. On the other hand, your offerings may be attractive to almost any industry, like office supplies, payroll processing and advertising. But even where industry is not necessarily a factor, most companies

tend to get their sales from a relatively limited number of industries, because those are the industries in which they have experience and can understand the needs of buyers.

3. Company Size. Your company will typically have the greatest success with either small, midsize or large companies. Sometimes this is a matter of matching your company to the size of your customers. Most big companies, for example, want to have a large, brand-name public relations firm when they face image problems. They want their vendor to have the same multiple layers of management that they themselves have. There's little practical justification for this, but it is by far the norm. Small companies, on the other hand, cannot usually afford big, brand-name PR flacks — and can also not get value from them, because the big vendor assigns its "farm team" to small companies. But there are also vendor-customer relationships in which small and midsize vendors *only* sell to big companies, because only big companies can afford what they sell. An example would be those companies that stage huge media productions at trade shows, which require budgets in the hundreds of thousands of dollars. The point is that, whatever rules govern your customer relationships, you will find that company size is a factor. The trick is to differentiate between the target markets where the size of your company is an advantage, and where it is not.

4. Department and Job Title. In most companies, there are three departments or job titles to which you sell: the direct buyer (typically in middle to senior management), the purchasing department (which can be a barrier to the sale) and the buyer's boss or committee (to which the direct buyer ultimately must sell your solution). Sometimes, you get lucky: your direct buyer is the decision-maker, and there's no purchasing department to worry about. But in most cases, your marketing and sales effort aims to persuade the direct buyer, but also to head off problems with the purchasing

department and to equip your direct buyer to sell for you inside the company.

That's complicated enough. But there's more. What you sell may be superb solution for one person in a company — and a serious threat to the job security of another. So your choice of direct buyer is vital. There are few more effective ways to waste your time than trying to sell a mailroom outsourcing service to the head of the mailroom. Likewise, sales force automation products are hot sellers — but very few sales professionals like them, because they take the salesperson's Rolodex and turn it into the property of the company, thereby reducing the individual salesperson's leverage. So closing a software deal with the head of sales may be more challenging than it appears.

5.   Need Fulfillment. This is the most subtle and vital of all. What does this target group need from you? Is it the same as other customers? What do you have to change about your business in order to meet these needs? Just as you do it for your existing customers, you need to define the value proposition (see page 20) for any new target group, and to base your sale on a careful analysis of needs. We will discuss this latter point in the Sales section beginning in Chapter 12.

Targeting for the IT Outsourcer

It's time to take up again the story of our IT outsourcing client, which we introduced on pages 14 and 17. This high-volume print-and-distribution company faced two challenges. Price pressure from competitors was eroding its margins, and its core customer group of IT managers was ceding influence over the buying decision to new players in marketing and customer service.

Since this chapter is on targeting, you have probably already guessed that their problem contained the seeds of opportunity. (The Chinese character for "crisis," we are told, is composed of the characters for "problem" and "opportunity.") If their traditional target group was losing influence, it raised the possibility that a new addressable target group — marketing and customer service executives — was emerging.

We interviewed a set of these new customers and potential buyers, and we learned that they had needs very different from the IT or technology operations executive. For them, print-and-distribution was not a necessary evil, as it was for the IT department. It was an issue that was core to their mission. It was about customer satisfaction and corporate image. It was about saving money by reducing the number of calls from confused people to the customer service line. It was about the opportunity to bundle new services into their offering or achieving a competitive advantage in a crowded market.

So far so good. Then we discovered something even better. They were unsophisticated buyers. (See page 27.) They knew nothing about pre-print processing, Group One software and Pitney Bowes Series 8 inserters. What they did know what how their invoice or statement had to look, what features it had to contain, and how fast it had to get there. They were willing to rely on vendors to make it happen.

Based on these interviews, we told our client that they were facing, not a threat, but a significant opportunity. Here was a group of buyers with urgent needs, a high degree of frustration with corporate IT for not meeting them, and rising influence over the purchasing decision.

Thinking in Circles

Before we finish the story, we need to go a little deeper into the *practice* of targeting. Because it makes a great deal of difference *how* you apply the criteria to your markets. For example, your company may have lots of midsize customers in your geographic area. But you may also have some small company customers. Maybe you also serve one or two industrial giants on the other side of the country. Are you supposed to just forget about these in your targeting decisions?

By no means. The point of this targeting exercise is to set clear priorities that allow salespeople to recognize a good prospect and to sell pro-actively without wasting time on random wandering. You may have a giant industrial company on the far side of the country as a customer — but odds are this is a happy accident. If you tried to build a business on this kind of customer, you'd go broke fast. So you don't want your salespeople focusing on it when there are much better prospects out there.

It is useful to think of your market as a set of concentric circles. The **Inner Circle** contains the companies most likely to buy from you. And who are they? They're companies that most closely resemble the biggest group of your existing customers, as defined by the five targeting factors we listed above.

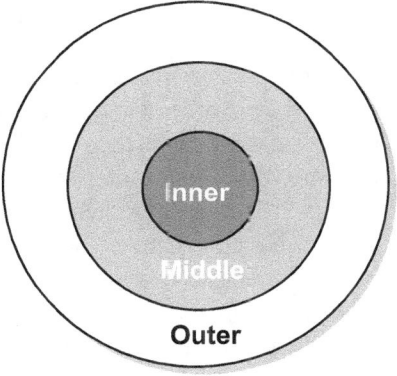

In the example of our teleport client, the broadcast and cable industry occupied their Inner Circle.

The **Middle Circle** contains companies that have potential but have not yet proven themselves as lucrative as the members of your Inner Circle. The members of the Middle Circle are typically companies that are like the exceptions on your customer list: the small companies in your geographic area, the industrial giants far away, all the customers you have that do not fit into the Inner Circle. These anomalies may be happy accidents — one-time buyers that did not return — but they may also be industries, geographic areas, or personality types that could provide sales growth if properly cultivated.

You won't know until you devote some energy to finding out. For our teleport client, foreign ISPs were in the Middle Circle, but they wound up producing enough business to become part of the Inner Circle — which is the engine that causes companies to grow.

The **Outer Circle** contains companies that ought to be buyers but are not. We have all looked at industries or company types and thought, "Our products and services are perfect for these guys! Why don't they buy from us?" In most cases, there are valid reasons why they haven't become customers — you just haven't found out yet what they are. But sometimes, these buyer groups are an untapped resource that will respond to a sales and marketing campaign. While working for the teleport operator, we tried to develop business in satellite-based videoconferencing. The teleport operator occasionally set up a videoconference for a trade association or public relations firm, connecting several dozen sites by video over satellite. This business tended to walk in the door by itself. When we tried to actively develop more of it — talking to past buyers, developing a pilot service offering and coaching a salesperson in trying to sell it — we got nowhere. They weren't buying, except in the rare cases when they did, and marketing to them did not change things a bit. Without being able to say why — and figuring that it wasn't worth more time and money to find out — we consigned videoconferencing customers to the operator's Outer Circle.

Allocating Your Resources

There are few things more discouraging than trying to sell to the wrong customer. Once you have your market organized in this way, you and your salespeople will be able to allocate your time much more productively, and feel much less frustrated at the same time. As a rule of thumb, your company should devote 60% of its selling resources to the Inner Circle, 30% to the Middle Circle, and 10% to the Outer Circle. That's a rough gauge based on our experience, and your own market may require a different allocation. The percentages will also shift depending on where you are in the economic cycle; recessions can be good times to focus more resources on your Middle and Outer Circle, because in bad times, potential customers are second-guessing their customary way of doing things. In good times, your Inner Circle may provide all the growth you can handle.

Finally, be sure to remember that targeting is not a fixed thing. You should review your company's targeting at least every 12 months. Some of the prospective customers in your Middle Circle may have converted into customers. Some may be in new industries that seem to offer potential. Maybe they bought a new service or product you are offering that suits them better than previous ones. At the same time, your Inner Circle may have found a more cost-effective solution than you are currently offering. In that fluid, dynamic thing we call a market, no decision can ever be considered final, and no range of targets will ever remain the same for long.

CHAPTER 5

Price Pointers

The operational approach to pricing is to cover our costs and produce a profit. The marketing approach to pricing is to get *more*. That is, to persuade buyers to spend more money for our offerings because of the higher value they perceive those offerings to have.

Marketing is vital to a business because it is one means of building perceived value and thereby charging more. The other means is innovation, by which we create something new that meets a need and for which we can charge a premium price because, for a period of time, we are the only supplier on the planet. Actually, innovation alone is never enough, because innovations are quickly spotted and imitated or improved upon by competitors (except in specialized industries such as pharmaceuticals, where patents rule). Effective marketing extends the period of time during which the company can maintain a sufficiently dominant position for its innovations to exercise control over pricing.

Once our products or services face lots of look-alike competition from other companies, pricing power is lost. Instead of innovations, we have a handful of commodities. We face relentless downward pressure on prices. The winner is then the company that can produce and deliver the product or service at the lowest cost, and has sufficient capital to outlast its competitors in a price war.

Keeping it Simple, Stupid

Pricing can become hugely complex. Many B2C companies, from airlines to retailers, have invested in sophisticated computer software to manage prices on an hour-by-hour or minute-by-minute basis. Generally speaking, B2B sales are so much larger in value and occur so much less frequently than B2C sales that there's only so much a piece of software can add to human decision-making.

Getting tricky with pricing, however, can have one major unintended consequence. It can really piss off the customer. Ask passengers what they think of airline ticket pricing, which is managed by some of the most sophisticated "yield management" systems on earth. The result is that a seat may cost $200 one day and $2,000 the next. Passengers hate it and have begun flocking to competitors like Southwest Airlines and RyanAir that offer simple, transparent pricing. When Amazon.com experimented with a variable pricing program for books that based the price on the demographic profile of the customer, it ran into a firestorm of criticism and promptly dropped the program. If my annual income is bigger than yours, does that mean I should pay $2 more for a book? Marketers and salespeople face a never-ending temptation worthy of Adam and Eve: thinking they are smart enough to manipulate customers without being found out. It can work. But sooner or later, customers figure it out, and their anger can last a long time.

Getting More for Outsourced IT Services

We ended our last installment of the IT outsourcing story with the discovery that our client faced, not a threat, but a new target market. And best of all, this market was made up of unsophisticated buyers who might well perceive a higher value in the company's solutions.

The client's response to our report was truly impressive. They quickly decided to invest in developing a software package that could take customer data in just about any format and process it to produce bills and statements with the features that the marketing and customer service people were demanding. This wasn't rocket science. Essentially, the company front-loaded and standardized work that it had previously done on a custom basis for each customer — adding weeks of delay to the start of service — and built in every bell and whistle it could think of. Standardization meant a higher upfront cost. But this technology innovation provided advantages that marketing and sales could exploit: fast start-up, a pre-packaged set of attractive features, and demonstrated expertise.

We were able to brand this new package as a "statement processing service" and truthfully claim that it was unique.

We developed a new set of features and benefits designed to appeal to executives in marketing and sales rather than IT.

We trained the salespeople to stop selling plain vanilla print-and-distribute services and, instead, to target marketing and customer service executives and sell to their needs.

We did an official launch of the service with all of the marketing razzmatazz and kept up a barrage of communications to the client's target industries for 18 solid months.

And how did the company price this branded service? Again, no rocket science was involved. They used their standard pricing models that accounted for personnel time. They included time charges for their computer (CPU) and per-unit charges for their printers and mailing equipment that had been developed to cover both consumables and depreciation. They factored in overhead, payback of their upfront investment in developing the package, and the profit margin they were able to get when not locked in head-to-head price competition with another vendor. The total averaged 14% higher than they had been able to charge for essentially the same bundle of services delivered in their former plain vanilla flavor. And they were able to get their price most of the time.

Within two years, this new statement processing service had doubled the company's historic rate of revenue growth and restored margins that had been eroded by pricing pressure. When the company went public a couple of years later, it attributed its success to the strong growth of its statement processing operations. It went on providing print-and-distribute service to IT departments, of course, but the company no longer viewed this as a core market and gained the luxury of being able to turn down business that did not meet its profitability standards.

Hail the Conquering Heroes

And so we were heroes, right? Well, it would be more accurate to say we walked in the company of heroes. By that time, the top managers had lived with this change of strategy long enough to make it their own. The sales team that was making it succeed in the field knew that the victories were their own doing. And that's the sign of a marketing job well done.

The rise of price pressure is a sign that what your company offers is turning into a commodity. The only solution is to offer something else. But that "something else" seldom requires a blind leap of faith. Instead, you are most likely to find it by taking an honest, clear-eyed look at your customers. Talking to them. Finding out how today's customers differ from yesterday's customers. The innovations that succeed are usually fairly small improvements on, or re-packaging of, what you already offer. They succeed because they meet new needs, often of a new group of customers, and most importantly, because you market them well, train your salespeople to sell them well, and deliver on the promises you make concerning quality, turnaround and overall value. If you do all of this, pricing pressure evaporates, because there is no comparable product or service to which yours can easily be compared.

B2B
Marketing
Tactics

Why B2B Isn't Like B2C

Advertising

Public Relations

Direct Marketing

The Web Site

Sales Support

CHAPTER 6

Why B2B Isn't Like B2C

For the decision-makers of most B2B companies, marketing decisions are an abyss of uncertainty. The sales representatives of industry magazines call and try to sell you space in their publications. Mailing list brokers push email and postal address lists at you. Telemarketers want to bird-dog new prospects for you. Web design firms want to retool or optimize or replace your Web site.

Who do you listen to? What's the magic mix that will bring more business in your door? And what makes these guys think you're going to spend *that* much on their services, anyway?

In the next few chapters, we're going to do two things. First, we're going to give you some rules of thumb for spending marketing dollars wisely in the B2B space. Then we're going to give you the story behind the rules: what your meaningful options really are, how to decide among them, and where there are exceptions to the rules that may apply to your situation. In the process, we'll introduce you to the basic marketing tools that really work in B2B.

Standing B2C On Its Head

What makes marketing so confusing for B2B managers? It's because most of the common wisdom about marketing that we learn in a class or absorb while doing business is based on selling to consumers. The B2B world turns most of this on its head, for a few simple reasons.

- In the B2C world, buyers are amateurs doing the work of purchasing in their spare time. In B2B, buyers are being paid to make the right choice for the organization.

- In the B2C world, buyers typically spend their money on low-priced products or services, so that a bad decision carries little risk. In the B2B world, the value of the purchase is typically high and a sufficiently bad decision can cost buyers their jobs.
- In B2C, the market consists of hundreds of thousands or millions of potential buyers. In the B2B world, the addressable market usually consists of only a few thousand potential customers.

Different, right? And so the techniques for getting your message out to this market and creating customers from it have to be different. The average B2B company needs a marketing mix that looks like the table in the next section.

Rules of Thumb

The table below is our starting point for designing a B2B marketing program for a client company. As such, it is not ideally suited for any particular company (and our lawyer will cheerfully give you two or three pages of "we're not liable for anything if you try this at home" statements). But it may serve to open your eyes to how different B2B marketing really is.

Tactics	Budget Allocation
Advertising Don't bother. With only a few thousand buyers, advertising is almost always a waste in B2B. There are exceptions, but in general, there are lots more productive ways to spend your money.	0%

Public Relations   20%

While advertising is typically uneconomic for B2B
marketers, public relations is a one of the best invest-
ments you can make. B2B markets are typically
small communities where the grapevine dominates
and both competitors and customers know each other.
PR — which includes press releases, editorial outreach to get you coverage in the trade press, and an
ongoing effort to place your executives as speakers at
industry events — is a low-cost method of influencing
what the grapevine is saying about your company.

Direct Marketing   20%

This category, also called lead-generation, sends out
messages to prospective customers and tries to motivate them to contact you. The methods include direct
mail, telemarketing, email broadcasts, fax broadcasts
and magazine or newspaper ads that make a special
offer and call for a response.

The Web Site   20%

The World Wide Web is the B2B marketer's dream.
At a fraction of the cost of traditional advertising or
direct marketing, it can create a public face for your
company, provide a forum for user groups, deliver
services, and underpin all your other marketing
efforts.

Sales Support   15%

In this category, we place brochures, PowerPoint
presentations, white papers and case studies,
networking events, and (a major budget item) trade
show exhibition.

Notice that the total budget allocation doesn't add up to 100%?
That's because we have purposely omitted an important cate-

gory: investment in developing new products or services, as with our story of the IT services firm. This is something that smart companies do 365 days a year, with time off only for holidays and extraordinarily good behavior. But it is also a topic that deserves an extended discussion to itself, whereas we want to focus in this book on the art of B2B selling.

Reputation, References and Referrals

Back in the early Nineties, the Gartner Group did a study of the reasons that information technology managers gave for buying from their current suppliers. We believe that this list applies to most non-commodity B2B buying decisions (excluding stuff like office supplies and railroad carloads of coal). The top three factors are (1) reputation, (2) referrals and (3) references. Price came in a distant fourth.

We hope that list makes you pause for a moment. More than anything else, your company's future will be determined by *what people in the market say about you*. Not your beautiful new offices, not the slick brochure, not the multimedia presentation. Just good old-fashioned word-of-mouth, extended by the instant, global communication tools of our Digital Age.

This striking fact guides our choice of things to spend marketing dollars on. We seek to spend money on activities that will polish your reputation, refer to successful solutions you have provided, and let your customer list speak for you. We prefer to showcase your knowledge rather than brag about your virtues. We seek to extend and deepen the natural relationships you have rather than hunt far and wide for potential buyers who have never heard of you. In the small world of most B2B markets, this is the way to spend as little as possible while earning the best possible return.

CHAPTER 7

Advertising

Advertising is the most expensive and indirect way to make contact with people you hope may be customers. Advertising means black-and-white ads in newspapers, glossy color magazine ads, 60-second commercials on radio or 30-second "spots" on TV. It's the first thing most business people think about when the subject of customer outreach comes up. And in our experience, it's completely inappropriate for the majority of B2B companies.

Why? Because of how expensive it is, and how indirectly it leads to a sale. Costs range from a few thousand dollars for creating the ad and buying space in newspapers or a trade journal, up to hundreds of thousands or millions of dollars for TV ads.

Paying that money gets you an opportunity — nothing more — to grab people's attention for a few seconds while they are doing something else, like reading an article, listening to music or watching a favorite show. Advertising tries to interest them, intrigue them, make them want something, or fear the consequences of not having it. People respond by ignoring it (most of the time) or by paying attention and, possibly, remembering the product/service and the message when they're at the point of sale. That's called building the brand, and it's what advertising does best. People are repeatedly exposed to a product or company name in an engaging way, and may even absorb some of the marketing message in the process. So when they have a closer encounter with that company or product — in a store, by mail or on the phone — they recognize it and may even have feelings about it: "it's so cool," or "it really works!"

That's what you're buying. To put this in perspective, the advertising agency Doyle Dane Bernbach did pioneering research decades ago and discovered that 80% of magazine readers will never read past the headline of an ad — your expensive, precious ad — even if the headline interests them.

Put that way, why would anybody spend money on advertising?

Because it works. We would not be so saturated with advertising messages each day if it didn't. But in order to work, advertising needs to be seen by the target audience many times. (Remember, they're doing their best to ignore it.) In order to accomplish that goal, you have to buy advertising space or time in lots and lots of media outlets for many days or weeks or months. That's why you see those commercials for McDonald's or Pepsi or GEICO insurance all over your dial night after night.

So — we have a very expensive medium to begin with, and a requirement to buy large quantities of it in order to have an impact. This explains why advertising is generally cost-effective only for mass audiences in the hundreds of thousands or millions of people. That does not describe very many B2B markets, where the number of potential buyers is typically less than five thousand.

B2B companies that lack experience with advertising tend to create an ad, run it one or two times, and then stop, overcome by sticker shock. They might just as well have run their dollars through a shredder.

Exceptions to the Rule

It wouldn't be a rule if there weren't exceptions. The most common exception is advertising in an industry directory or Yellow Pages. Here, the decision should be not whether to advertise but how much to spend and which opportunities will be most cost-effective. The advertising options themselves — ranging from bold or colored type to logo display to a box ad — are not particularly expensive. But there are typically lots of directories, directory issues of trade journals, Web listings and alternative Yellow Pages in your service areas. The costs can add up quickly unless you take a very rational approach to buying. But it's worth spending what you can afford to spend, because your bold listing or logo or ad reaches the potential buyer when he or she has a need and is preparing to spend money.

You should also at least consider advertising in the annual trade show issue of your industry's favorite journal. This issue will not just be mailed to subscribers but will also be distributed to everyone who attends the show. It is the issue where the largest number of your competitors will appear, and if you want to be considered a player in the market, it makes sense to buy an ad and include your booth number, if you are exhibiting there. It's not essential, but will tend to deliver greater value than most advertising opportunities.

Advertising is also a reasonable investment for the B2B company whose primary marketing objective is brand-building. This company's stock-in-trade may be its expertise, contacts and influence, such as a management consultant, professional service firm, medical practitioner or some niches in the financial services industry. Companies like these can't proactively sell their services; nobody wants to use an expert who brags about his connections and influence but has to chase ambulances to get business.

Or the business may need to be selective about the customers it chooses to serve, but lacks any objective means to qualify them except face-to-face. In this case, most other forms of marketing will be ineffective, and so advertising (and public relations, see below) must carry the load. A client company of ours is in the catastrophe reinsurance business, which means that it insures insurance companies against natural and manmade disasters for which the insurers have written policies. This company takes a counter-cyclical approach to the market. When its competitors are clawing each other for market share, this company tends to pull back from the market, because it can't get the prices it wants. When a string of disasters causes shell-shocked competitors to pay out huge sums and withdraw from writing more business, it plunges into the market. For this company, brand-building through advertising is a reasonable choice. It needs to be a well-known and trusted player yet, on average, the company turns away more business than it chooses to accept.

One clever marketer we know even goes so far as to create full-color, full-page magazine ads that never appear in a magazine. Instead, he reproduces a couple of thousand of each one and puts it into his sales literature. Prospective customers see them and assume the company is an advertiser, which conveys a "big company" image, while they are exposed to the marketing message at the point of sale. It's not orthodox marketing, but it delivers many of the benefits of advertising at a fraction of the cost.

What to Put in an Ad

Okay, so you have decided that one of our exceptions applies to your situation, and you are going to place an ad in the show guide of your industry's big convention. Heck, you're going to splurge and run ads as well in the daily newspaper that is placed outside the hotel room of every delegate.

So now, confronted by a blank piece of paper, what do you have to say?

We once faced this challenge for a company whose primary business was reupholstering bus seats. That's right: taking those spilled-on, cigarette-burned, baby-accident seats from Greyhound, commuter bus lines and even school bus companies and making them look brand spanking new.

Not a natural for breakthrough advertising.

We spent time talking to the client and, by phone, to one or two customers. And a theme emerged. Nobody could believe what absolute *pigs* the bus passengers were. It would take a true swine, a wild boar, a berserk herd of hogs, to do the kind of damage to these seats that the company saw every day.

Inspiration struck. We researched photos and came up with a truly beautiful shot of a pigsty at sunset, with warm autumnal light bathing the hogs and one adorable little piggy pushing its snout up to the lens. We wrote a headline, based on a quote from one of the company's clients, that asked the reader what the condition of his bus seats made him think of. Then we presented it to our client's small management team. The room broke up. They loved it. It was perfect.

It took less than 30 minutes for them to talk themselves out of it.

Somebody was sure to be upset, they said. We were insulting the bus company's customers. They couldn't afford to take the chance. Despite the fact that the ad would never be seen by passengers, despite the fact that it would have been the only ad any reader of the magazine remembered, it never saw the light of day.

As you think about your own advertising message, keep this little story in mind. In addition to the tips we offer you in the rest of the chapter, good advertising takes one more, very special ingredient: the courage to say something worth remembering.

WHAT TO DO

1. **Focus on One Idea.** An ad is not a catalog or report or laundry list. Nobody is getting paid to read it, and they'll give you only seconds of their time before moving on. So come up with one simple, powerful statement of who you are or what you offer that sets you apart. A great series of ads for a company that made construction equip-

ment was based on the single, powerful idea "More per hour." Every ad featured a photo of one of their machines hard at work on a building site, and explained how using it allowed the contractor to get more productivity from its hourly workers or reduce its hourly costs in some other way. Once the one, powerful idea caught the attention of readers, they were willing to read the rest of the ad to learn more.

2. **Think in Pictures.** What makes readers stop to look at an ad? Most of the time, it is a striking visual: an illustration or photo or graphic design. So when you create an ad, the visual element should not be an afterthought — it should be the kick-off point. Our favorite way to approach the creation of an ad is to come up with some themes or rough headlines expressing our one idea. (The headline is the large, boldface type at the top of most ads.) We then have our graphic designer research photographs that relate to those ideas. There are hundreds of "stock photo" companies and agencies representing photographers that can provide you with tens of thousands of existing images. These are usually much cheaper than original photography. When the designer presents his choices, we usually find one photo that is so striking, we know it will be the final choice, and we write the rest of the ad to go with it.

3. **Assume that Nobody Will Read Past the Headline.** As we reported earlier in this chapter, 80% of your readers will never read past the headline. So you need to write a headline that expresses your one idea in words that also tell people what the heck your company does. That way, even a quick scan of the headline will communicate something meaningful. If you just can't fit a clue to what you do in the headline without ruining it, look for opportunities to convey it visually, or create subheadings

in the rest of the ad that explain it. After the headline, the subheadings are the most-often-read part of advertising.

4. **Feel Free to Be Funny.** If you can make your ad entertaining as well as informative, your readers will be grateful. We all like a laugh, and humor creates a positive impression in reader's minds while making your ad stand out from the crowd. One of our favorite B2B ads — for a company that offered complete video production and editing facilities — featured a photo of a burly guy in shirtsleeves, sitting at a video editing console and pointing an aggressive finger at the camera. The headline said," Call me a button-pusher, and I'll punch your lights out." Their pitch? That the people on their staff were not just a bunch of technicians, but professionals who could improve the quality of everything you did there. Be warned, though: humor involves risk. The concerns of our bus-seat reupholsterer about the "Pigg es" ad we presented were not crazy by any means. Good advertising, like everything else in business, requires you to balance risk and reward. Take no risks and you should expect no reward; take a well-thought-out risk, and you may profit handsomely.

WHAT TO AVOID

1. **Imitation.** Ask most B2B executives to come up with advertising, and their first impulse is to look at the ads of their closest competitors and produce something that looks just like them. A big waste of money. What they produce is wallpaper, not advertising. Standard, unmemorable, and fitting right in. Whereas the point of advertising is to stand out, be memorable and not fit in. It is important to check out what your competition's advertising, but for the opposite reason: to make sure that your look and message are different.

2. **Empty Words.** Remember the advice from your high school English teacher about not using clichés — those time-honored expressions that have been so overused as to lose all impact? Phrases like "people serving people" and "working harder to serve you better." Cliches are one form of what we call empty words, written to make the writer (or the boss) feel better but conveying nothing of interest to the reader. Words like "industry leader," "cutting edge" and that wonder of the last technology boom, "Internet time." Go ahead and write them. You'll feel better. But then take a red pencil and cross them out. They insult the intelligence of your reader. They are static that obscures the information you actually want to convey. Once they're crossed out, you stand a better chance of seeing what you really want to say and then saying it clearly.

3. **Empty Visuals.** If your ad includes artwork that is merely decorative, get rid of it. The space you are buying is too expensive for Beaux Arts. How can you tell the difference between necessary and unnecessary visuals? First of all, a photo of your office building is always unnecessary. Who cares, except you and your realtor? But seriously, the easiest way to spot an unnecessary visual is to try deleting it. If the message of the ad doesn't suffer, then the photo or image wasn't necessary in the first place.

Working with an Ad Agency

Because advertising is a specialized discipline, B2B companies that decide to advertise may be well advised to hire an ad agency. These are people who can do it all: write the ad, find the visuals, design it, produce it in the formats required by trade journals, and get the material there on time.

The challenge of finding a good agency in B2B is that few agencies understand the niche you're in, and even fewer will take the time to understand your buyers and their needs. Especially if you're beating them up on the price of their services, which is nearly standard practice.

The best way to get good value is to hire an agency whose work you like and then stick with them until they learn your business. It can take a while and requires patience on your part. But it will pay off in advertising that communicates effectively with your marketplace.

CHAPTER 8

Public Relations

We come honestly by our dubious attitude to B2B advertising. We have created and placed a lot of it for clients in exciting businesses like industrial testing, asbestos abatement and insurance — usually against our better judgment and in spite of our recommendations to the client. We have also bought it for our own account, and seen just how hit-or-miss the results have been.

But the same years of experience have made us major fans of public relations. Because when it works, it reaches the very same broad audience an ad does at a fraction of the cost, with greater credibility than any advertisement possesses.

What Is It?

Public relations is one of the most misunderstood and unappreciated forms of marketing communications. Mention PR, and people think of that classic Burt Lancaster-Tony Curtis film, *The Sweet Smell of Success*. They use flattering terms like "flack." They think it's all about who you know at *The Times*. One of the legendary figures in PR was a guy named James S. Moran, who died in 2000 at the age of 91. Moran believed that PR was about getting attention for his client, no matter what it took. He once sat on an ostrich egg for 19 days to promote a book with the odd title "The Egg and I." The hatching of the ostrich made news around the world and helped the book reach the best-seller list. On another occasion, he decided to promote a client's products by using kites to fly midgets over Central Park. Understandably, NYPD refused him a permit for this bold experiment in aviation. But undeterred, Moran called the newspapers to complain. He was soon quoted in the press, with lavish references to his client, saying, "It's a sad day for capitalism when a man can't fly a midget on a kite over Central Park."

We love the Moran legend, but we probably wouldn't hire him. Because PR isn't generally about crazy stunts. It's a systematic way to shape how the market perceives your company. And it's based on the startling fact that over 70% of the news you read or hear comes, almost unedited, from company news releases. In the B2B space, the percentage is even higher. As a player in your market, your company has an outstanding opportunity to influence how your prospects, customers and competitors view the issues of the day, and we think you'd be crazy to miss it.

How It Works

Now, to the details. What is public relations and how does it work? In the B2B space, a PR program involves the following elements, all carefully coordinated:

1. PR Strategy

What do you want to accomplish? Whatever it is, we can guarantee you that it's not the most frequently-cited goal, which is "to get our name out there." The actor Hugh Grant got his name out there when he was caught picking up a lady of the evening shortly before he was to marry the stunning and talented Elizabeth Hurley —and thereby won the Shoot Yourself in the Foot award for 1995. Presumably this isn't the kind of context in which you want your name "out there."

Setting a PR strategy means deciding what perception you want your marketplace to have of your company. The first and most important rule is that this perception must be well grounded in reality. Microsoft tries valiantly to create the perception that its only concern is to create great software — but having been named a predatory monopolist by the US Justice Department and a Federal court, it doesn't have a snowball's chance in hell of being believed. Your company's actions are always going to speak louder than its words. So the perception you seek to create should be based on your actual strengths, not a hopeful fantasy. As Abraham Lincoln so ably noted, nobody is smart enough to fool all of the people all of the time.

The art of public relations is to tie your real strengths to the current concerns of your marketplace, so as to position your company in a positive light. Here's an example of how it can work.

We spent several years working for the largest wholesaler of heating, ventilating and air-conditioning (HVAC) equipment in the country. Not exactly a sexy business, though fundamental to the daily comfort of millions. Their customers were HVAC contractors, from one-man shops to large regional operators. Our client played the classic middleman role, buying in large quantities at volume discounts from the major suppliers, and offering its customers ready availability of an enormous number of items at market prices. The roots of the company went back decades, and the management knew their business. The margins between buying and selling prices were relatively static, so the name of the game was efficiency and being careful to buy only what would sell.

What was going on in the industry at the time? We talked to the client's executives, read the trade press and consulted with their regional warehouse executives. The top story of the day — and likely to be the top story for some time — was the phase-out of refrigerants containing chlorofluorocarbons (CFCs).

These were the nasty compounds that had been shown to destroy ozone in the upper atmosphere, which shields the surface of the earth from ultraviolet radiation. At the time, there were headlines every year about the annual opening of the "ozone hole" over Antarctica, which let unfiltered UV radiation reach the polar zone. To address this problem, the world's industrial nations had agreed to phase out products containing

CFCs, with refrigerants at the top of the list. The deadline was less than 18 months from the start of work for the wholesaler.

The trouble was that CFCs were the refrigerants used in residential and commercial air-conditioning systems, with names like CFC-12 and CFC-14. DuPont, the major refrigerant manufacturer, had come up with ozone-friendly replacements which it was pushing hard at the market, almost salivating in public over the anticipated surge of revenues and profits. (Naturally, the replacements were more expensive than the old CFC standbys, as well as being less efficient.)

In this kind of situation, the marketplace was overwhelmed with FUD (fear, uncertainty and doubt, to steal a phrase from the software industry). We realized that our client had the potential to benefit significantly from it, because in these uncertain times, their customers were looking for answers, and our client had them. In other words, we had an opportunity to create the perception that our client was a thought leader in the industry, the people who were helping the industry move confidently into a better future. In many ways, they were better positioned to do it than DuPont, the real expert, because DuPont's commercial incentives were so enormous.

2.   Newsgathering

Despite the common wisdom, companies don't make news because their PR flack is best buddies with an important editor. Companies make news — and editors keep their jobs — because they have something newsworthy to report. Once you know what your strategy is, you need to work on developing an ongoing stream of newsworthy information to feed the media machine.

What's newsworthy varies from industry to industry and from year to year. But there are a few tried-and-true categories:

- <u>Hiring of New Executives</u>. When you make a hire in the senior ranks, be sure to issue a press release about it. It lets the world know you are expanding.

- <u>Contract Awards</u>. When you win a job, even if it's a contract renewal, announce it. This tells the market that your company is growing even more dramatically than does a hiring announcement. Yet it never fails to amaze us how few companies take advantage of the opportunity. Some cite confidentiality clauses that customers demand in the contract. Others fear that competitors will zero in on the new customer and take away the business. Still others, though they would never admit it, feel that an announcement will somehow jinx the business. None of these reasons is compelling. You should include in your standard contract a clause that specifically authorizes you to announce the contract and name the customer; this will at least be a good starting point for negotiation. And if you are that fearful of competitors, or of attracting the evil eye — well, just how poor an opinion do you have of your company and its products and services?

- <u>Strategic Alliances</u>. If you have established a cross-marketing relationship, joint venture or operational alliance with another company, by all means alert the media. Even if the alliance goes nowhere — as most of them unfortunately do — it communicates the growth message.

- <u>New Products and Services</u>. If you roll out a new product, service or way of doing things, it's a perfect opportunity to promote your company. Even more, it's an essential form of support for the change.

Most B2B companies win a relatively small number of big-ticket accounts each year, and update their products and services all too seldom. Thus, there isn't that much natural news to report. In this case, you need to make your own — by researching and publishing data that will interest the market and position your company the way it wants to be seen.

Thus, our HVAC wholesaler client. Since we had decided, with the client's approval, to make them the CFC phase-out experts, we looked for news that would sell this message. Our client had hired some employees for its customer service center who had experience in converting CFC systems to run the new non-CFC refrigerants. That was news we could use. The client signed a deal with DuPont that would ensure it a ready supply of the new refrigerants even though they would be in high demand. More news we could use. By making the client attuned to the public relations benefit of these moves, we made it easier for the client to produce more of this news.

3.   Press Release.

The most basic instrument for communicating news to the media is the press release. The writing of press releases is a journalistic skill that we lack space to teach in full. But we can address a few of the more common errors that B2B companies commit:

- The first paragraph should contain a concise statement of your story — the big idea — written to intrigue readers so that they will keep reading. In the news business, they call it "Who, What When Where, Why and How."

- A press release is not an ad or brochure. Resist the urge to write promotional copy. Avoid like the plague those self-serving marketing phrases "leading company," "top-selling" and "breakthrough product." These are red flags to editors that your release is puffery, not news.

- Include a quote by your CEO or other top executive and, if possible, a quote by your customer or other third party. A statement by your CEO gives the news a certain added importance, which is valuable to your company and its investors. It also creates name recognition for your CEO, which can be a major asset in the industry, and offers valuable free publicity to your customer or ally.

- Don't forget to include the date of the announcement and the name, telephone number and email address of somebody at your company whom the press can contact for more information. Of course, nobody would be dumb enough to leave these out, right? Except the writers of about 10% of the releases we see.

Even more important than what you say is who you choose to say it to. A great deal of thought and care should go into the compiling of your press list. You can use one of the commercial sources — the Standard Rate and Data Service, Bacon's or other — to get contact information for the trade press in your industry. You should also include on the list:

- Local and state media that report on business, including radio and television as well as the more traditional newspapers and business journals

- Consultants and research companies that cover your industry

- The publications departments of the trade associations in your industry

- Your prospective customers (you will not actually add prospects to your press list, but rather, send press releases to your marketing and sales database)

You can distribute press releases by snail mail, but the common practice now is to distribute by email, preferably, or by fax where email addresses are lacking. It's faster and cheaper than the Post Office, and email in particular allows editors to pick up text direct from your release using the cut-and-paste function on their computer.

The initial press list for our wholesaler consisted of the surprisingly large number of trade journals that go to HVAC contractors, general contractors and real estate executives. There were a handful of national magazines, but a much larger number of regional or state newsletters and magazines, many of them published by trade associations. Going further, we identified the local or state business journals published wherever our client had branches.

A press list starts out as a database of publication contact information, with the title "Editor" but no individual names. (The commercial sources such as Bacon's often include editors' names but there is sufficient churn in editorial positions that you are safer sticking with the title.) The list gains value over time as you add information on individual editors gained in the next step.

4. Editorial Outreach. Editorial outreach is to PR what selling is to your company — the place where the feet meet the street. In fact, editorial outreach is nothing more or less than selling your company and your story to the editorial community. It takes the same skills as sales — the ability to truly listen and a gift for persuasion — but also requires an understanding of what makes news and the creativity to take what you hear from an editor and shape it into a story idea that the editor can use. It takes a lot of hours on the phone, a lot of email, and a lot of time reading the trade press so that you know what the hot buttons are at the moment.

Editorial outreach for the HVAC wholesaler began with selection of a small group of the national HVAC journals that we thought would have the greatest influence. We then checked the editorial calendars — available from their advertising media kits — to see what issues would cover the CFC deadline. After calling to determine who the appropriate editor would be for a story related to CFCs, we sent an introductory fax accompanied by background information on our client. We followed this up by phone, explained the client's position on the CFC issue, and inquired about contributing to a particular story on the editorial calendar.

Then, as in a sales situation, it was time to both listen carefully and think creatively. Most business editors or reporters are deeply interested in the topics they cover. They are willing to talk to anyone who can contribute something meaningful to their store of knowledge. They also run a journalistic machine that must be constantly fed with content. If what you have to say represents a solution to a problem, offers insight on a situation, or in any other way is useful to readers, they will want to know more.

The first tangible result of these conversations came in the form of "pick-up" of our press releases, meaning that a paragraph or two appeared in the News Briefs sections of the magazines, or news contained in the releases was quoted in longer feature stories. One of the journals had a major CFC story planned for an issue 3 months ahead; we arranged for the editor to interview one of our client's executives, and two quotes appeared in the issue. As we kept up the flow of information and outreach, the editors began to contact us when they needed a quote or piece of information on CFCs and had a deadline right around the corner. By responding fast and, with the client's help, providing useful input, we further solidified relationships with the media.

5.   Newsmaking. Working for the HVAC wholesaler, we milked the CFC story as long and hard as we could. But eventually, we hit the deadline for CFC phase-out. Controversy and concern continued for a few more months, but eventually everyone adjusted to the new reality and the journals lost interest in the topic. Under these circumstances, what's a PR professional to do?

When natural topics are few and far between, it's time to try making your own news. For the wholesaler, we went back to one of their core strengths: ongoing investment in technology and systems to make their operation more efficient, maintain their margins and better serve their customers. Having established the company as a "source" for the trade media, we thought we might be able to sell the company itself as a story. With the client's approval, we introduced an "Into the Future With Us" theme. The idea was that our client was investing to help bring HVAC contractors into the future in terms of product availability, ordering and delivery. Instead of CFCs, our press releases announced new systems the client had recently installed to expand their capacity or simplify ordering. We reached out to editors and pitched the "Into the Future" story. And we got results. The one that came with the biggest bragging rights was a cover story in the industry's leading journal about our client and their new multi-million-dollar regional distribution facility with all the bells and whistles imaginable.

You can make your own news by publishing white papers on important issues in your industry. You can contribute letters to the editor. Poll a small sample of your customers on the future of the industry or some burning issue, and put out a press release on the results. The possibilities are limited only by your imagination — so long as what you develop is firmly based on your strategy and relates to the needs and interests of the media as you have learned them through editorial outreach.

Return on Your Investment

So after all this time and effort, what do you get? For the HVAC wholesaler, our two years of work produced editorial coverage in industry trade journals, the regional business press and local television worth over $480,000. The cost to the client in fees and materials was less than 20% of that value.

And because the client's appearances in print were editorial rather than advertising, they had a credibility that no paid advertising can ever achieve.

How did we measure the value? It was based on the retail advertising cost of equivalent space in the publications, multiplied by a factor of 2 to represent its greater credibility. We could make the case that a multiple of 2 actually sells short the value of repeated editorial mention in the publications that your customers read most often. But if you prefer to eliminate the multiple, a value of $240,000 was still more than twice the cost of the PR investment.

We hope that we have made the case for the power and cost-effectiveness of well-executed PR. It is something you can do yourself, if you have the right in-house talent, or you can choose to hire a PR professional. If you go outside, plan to devote serious time and attention to selection. A shocking number of PR people, in our experience, have the same basic ideas about PR as Jim Moran — but only a fraction of his memorable (and shameless) creative talent.

CHAPTER 9

Direct Marketing

Direct marketing (DM) means finding a way to motivate prospective customers to contact *you*. It's one step short of knocking on their door yourself. The methods vary but all share a common theme: you send out a marketing message designed to appeal to people likely to buy from you, and they self-select themselves as your prospective customers. Another name for it is lead-generation. The most typical methods include:

In Trade Journals

- Small (usually quarter-page or less) ads that make a specific offer and provide an 800 number, email address or Web URL for response

- Those annoying blow-in cards that fall out of magazines when you open them, which also make an offer and provide a means to respond

- Bound-in inserts or cover wraps that do the same

By Mail

- Personalized business letters in a personalized envelope with Business Reply Card (BRC) or Envelope (BRE), which looks from the outside to be normal correspondence

- Non-personalized letters, typically with an offer in bright colors on the outside envelope and the recipient's address appearing through a window, with a BRC or BRE for response

- Self-mailers formed from a single large sheet of paper that is folded, perforated and glued to form its own envelope, with the offer in bright colors on the outside, typically addressed with an outside label (Cheshire or pressure-sensitive) and with a perforated BRC for response

- Postcards addressed with a Cheshire or pressure-sensitive label

Electronic

- Telemarketing, which uses low-level employees or an outside service company to telephone potential customers and make them an offer

- Email, either plain text or formatted using HTML coding, so that it resembles a Web page, with email and Web links back to you

- Fax broadcast, which is typically not personalized but can be made so using database technology

What Works in B2B?

For our money, the most cost-effective vehicles for B2B direct marketing are the personalized business letter, the postcard and email.

Personalized Business Letters. We like the personalized business letter because it is most likely to get opened and expose your message to the reader, whereas most of us toss out junk mail unopened. That said, you have to do it right. This means, first of all, carrying the personalization all the way through. The outer envelope must look like business correspondence, so no address labels or window envelopes can be used. You must send it first-class mail, and some marketers even like to have stamps individually applied, though we're a bit dubious of the value in the B2B space, where most companies have postage machines for their correspondence. The letter must be personalized as well. The tone and style of the letter must be business-like, friendly, and not too pushy. And you need to offer the reader some reason to keep reading and to respond. (More about the offer below).

The personalized business letter can be very effective, but it doesn't come cheap. You will pay somewhere between $1.50 and $2.00 to get an envelope into each recipient's hands. For that, the common wisdom of the industry says that you can anticipate a response rate of about 1%. (It used to average 2% but recipients are savvier these days.) Response rate, by the way, means the return of a reply card, a telephone call or email reply — not a sale. So by spending $150-200, you're going to get one lead on average. Is it worth the money? It depends on the revenue potential of that lead, and on your gross margin.

For one client, we created a small-scale lead-generation program using personalized mailings. Once a month, we wrote a new one-page letter and sent it, with BRC, to a list of about 1,000 publishing company contacts who were prospective buyers of our client's software. The response rate varied widely from month-to-month but averaged slightly more than 2%. The client's VP of Sales — who was also the only sales-person — followed up by phone and tried to get appointments with the respondents. It wasn't fancy, but after a few months, it was running like a well-oiled machine. Which was when the client announced, with regret, that he was terminating the program. Why? Because he had just closed a really big deal with one of the respondents to our program. And so he didn't need to advertise any more.

(Hey folks, we just report the news. We don't pretend to understand it.) At least the guy served as an enthusiastic reference for our firm for many years thereafter

Postcards. We like the postcard because the message is in plain sight — almost everyone will at least flip over a post-card to see what it says — and it's cheap. Rather than being individually personalized, they are printed in bulk and addressed with inexpensive labeling machines. You send them out at third-class bulk rate. Your total costs to reach one recipient will be in the 40-60¢ range, less than 1/3 of the personalized business letter. The response rate will average 0.25-0.50%. This makes it potentially more cost-effective than the business letter, though it obviously offers less space to communicate your message, and requires you to mail out larger volumes in order to achieve a meaningful result.

Email. We're also fond of B2B email marketing. It's even cheaper — if you use one of the many low-cost services on the Web and use your own list, it will cost you as little as $300-400 *per year*. It reaches people right at the desktop, something that fax broadcasting can't do. Of course, most people delete unsolicited email without reading more than the headline — the response rate is one-tenth of 1% (0.01%) or less — but the minimal cost means that you can live with a low response rate.

Unsolicited email, or "spam," became a significant consumer issue for the first time in 2003, when some email service, providers, including Microsoft and Earthlink, estimated that as much as 40% of email traffic on the Internet was spam. While technology companies created defenses and Congress introduced anti-spam legislation, honorable direct marketers tried to decide how to respond. Fortunately, the rules of the road for email marketing are pretty simple. The basic premise is that recipients have to have the right to opt out — and stay out — of the marketer's distribution list. We recommend the following approach to B2B direct marketers:

1. Some consumer advocates believe there should be *no* unsolicited email, or at most, that marketers should contact recipients and request their permission to send future emails. We think this is unrealistic. In the world of snail-mail, no one expects marketers to send a letter requesting permission to send junk mail. Why? Because people do not generally perceive that the junk mail they receive

does them great harm. They just toss out the stuff that's of no interest. Spam is a bit more annoying because there's so much of it. But in email as in snail-mail, we believe that it's ethical and reasonable to assume the recipient is willing to receive your email until you hear otherwise.

2. The corollary of this position is that you must make it easy for people to tell you to stop emailing them. An "unsubscribe me" message at the end of your email, which contains a link that generates an out-bound email to you, will do the trick.

3. When you receive one of those "unsubscribe me" emails, you must immediately mark that contact in your database in some way that ensures no future email marketing goes to that person. In other words, you have to keep the promise you make in your unsubscribe message. You can go one better by not only arranging for the person not to receive email from you, but by sending an email thanking them for contacting you and confirming that they have been removed from the email list. That way, you have a chance to make a good impression on a business contact who may not want email from you but might still have a need you can satisfy.

What do you say in your unsolicited email? Rule #1 is: *don't be spam.* With spam wasting so much Internet bandwidth, companies and individuals are implementing spam-blocking software that analyzes messages for spam tendencies and allows users to place particular sender's addresses on an "enemies" list. So with one click of a mouse, your email to a particular recipient can be permanently consigned to the waste bin (unless you follow in the footsteps of the true spammers and send from a new bogus address every time).

Not being spam means writing professional business correspondence, light on the fancy graphic effects, that makes a useful offer. Make sure your "from" address is a normal, valid email address, and that your "subject" line avoids advertising "come-on" language and simply states your purpose. These are the same principles you would apply to sending personalized business letters, based on respect for the intelligence of the recipient.

What Doesn't Work in B2B?

What about the other stuff on our list? For every form of direct marketing, you can find successful case studies. But for most B2B companies most of the time, we have not found the other stuff to be as consistently cost-effective and affordable.

For example, brightly colored outer envelopes and self-mailers deliver great results — sometimes. But they are expensive to design and produce. Our experience with B2B clients has been that the expense is great enough to cause cold feet. We may do one mailing or even two, but then the mounting cost causes the client to stop — effectively wasting the investment to date. The most extreme case was the company that paid us to create and print 20,000 copies of a full-color self-mailer, only to cancel the project before we could get it into the mail.

The same applies to magazine-based direct marketing. Because advertising — whether in the pages of the magazine or via blow-in card — is costly, there's a relatively steep price to get into the game. And as with all advertising, you can't just do it once but need to keep spending month after month.

The same applies, doubly, to telemarketing. It's really expensive: $15-25 per hour for a trained telemarketer to attempt 15-20 calls and maybe complete one interview.

Let's be clear about what we mean by telemarketing. This is not telephone cold-calling by a B2B salesperson, or having a sales assistant call companies, identify the most likely buyer and gather a little pre-qualification data. Those are the basic blocking-and-tackling of B2B sales. Telemarketing, on the other hand, is a self-contained effort to complete a sale over the phone. Properly designed telemarketing programs can yield good results — otherwise, your dinner hour would not be interrupted so often — but the B2B world presents unique obstacles. There are company operators and administrative assistants to get past, and the ubiquitous use of voicemail. The people on the other end of the phone are usually busy and may find it annoying to talk to a low-level employee reading from a script. (We certainly do.) In our experience, it doesn't justify the expense and trouble involved.

And fax broadcasting? Back in the pre-email days, it used to work about as well as email marketing does now. But today, the fax machine is off in a corner or in the mail room and a clerical employee typically tosses the "junk" before it can ever reach a decision-maker. If you're selling something that people in the mailroom might buy, it's perfect. Or if you send personalized faxes, looking like real business correspondence, it can sometimes work, because it is more likely to reach the recipient. Otherwise, don't bother.

Elements of a Successful Campaign

The scary thing about DM is that you can select one of our favorite vehicles, spend your money, and get nothing. Or you can get a great response rate. There are three variables that you need to get right in order to succeed. One is selecting a cost-effective vehicle appropriate to your message and market, as discussed above. The other two are:

- **The List.** If the quality of the list is good (meaning that it is up-to-date) and it is well-targeted (meaning that the needs of the people on the list are a good match for what you're selling), you've got a winning combination.

- **The Offer.** The key to DM is action. Your solicitation needs to make an offer that is both desirable and simple, so that there is a good chance of your reader responding within 30-60 seconds after he or she finishes reading. If your offer isn't desirable, you won't succeed. If your offer is complicated or involves the weighing of risks, you won't succeed. If you don't make an offer but only try to persuade, you're dead.

The importance of these three variables can't be over-emphasized. Like death and taxes, they are the unavoidable determiners of your life as a B2B direct marketer. The following rules should guide you in juggling the variables:

1. **The Only Good List is One You've Tried.** When you rent a direct marketing list, assume the worst and you'll be right most of the time. There is only so current the best DM list can be, because they are drawn from sources — magazine circulation, Yellow Pages, association memberships — that are themselves months behind the fast changes of modern life. And very few lists are "the best." So you won't know how good the list is for your purposes until you've tried it.

2. **If You Don't Have an Offer, Invent One!** The ideal DM product or service is low-cost and low-risk. It's an impulse-purchase item. It's a Ginzu Knife ("as seen on TV!") But how many B2B products or services fit this description? Darned few. They tend to be big-ticket items with high value that carry risks to the buyer in proportion to that value. So a B2B direct marketer needs to break down the big proposition into something bite-sized. Rather than trying to sell your product or service, "sell" a free research report. Offer an online demo or free

trial. Come up with a low-cost, no-risk variation on your products or services and offer that as an introduction. A top-performing salesman once said to us, "My goal at the first meeting is not to sell my product. It's to sell a second meeting." The same principle applies here.

3. **Test, Test, Test.** Just as with advertising, you are better off shredding your dollars than doing one direct mailing and then giving up. Because you don't know which list will work, or what offer will be most welcome, you have to test and keep testing. You must be rigorous and scientific about it. You can only test one variable at a time. Try sending out the same offer to several different lists. The one that gets the best response becomes your "control" list. Now try different offers to that same "control" list. The one that gets the best response is your "control" offer. Now you may want to try different DM vehicles using your "control" list and offer. The one that performs best... But you get the idea. And remember that nothing stands still. New list sources will come to your attention. Somebody on your team will come up with a different offer. In each case, you test it — one variable at a time — against your "control." If the list or offer produces better results, it becomes the new "control."

Not For Sissies

Still with us after all that? One thing should be clear to you: direct marketing isn't for sissies. You need to think it through carefully — knowing that you don't yet know very much — and then commit time and money to a consistent effort. The pay-off comes when your direct marketing is getting responses greater than the average, and produces a flow of qualified leads that transform into strong revenue growth.

CHAPTER 10

The Web Site

The World Wide Web is the greatest gift to B2B sales and marketing since the invention of the trade show. Dollar-for-dollar, the Web delivers more value to the B2B marketer than any other marketing vehicle. Here's why:

- **Low Cost.** A Web site can make your company look good for far less than you would spend on any brochure or flyer. Not only is the cost of entry low, but the deal keeps getting better. Because you can update your Web site constantly for a fraction of the cost of revising and reprinting traditional marketing materials.

- **High "Touch."** Thanks to hyperlinking — the ability of a link in an email or other Web site to take the user to a specific part of your Web site — you can get better information to potential customers far faster than ever before.

- **Better, Cheaper Service.** The same hyperlinking allows prospects and customers to respond instantly via email. Depending on what your company does, you may also be able to answer many common (prospective) customer questions with information already on the site. If your business involves providing people with forms, manuals, software downloads or other material suitable for electronic distribution, you can provide an online self-service "kiosk" to site visitors at little cost.

- **E-Commerce.** And then there's the actual sale of stuff to customers over the Internet. Unfortunately, few B2B businesses are naturals for e-commerce. The sweet spot for e-commerce tends to be in the sale of relatively commoditized, low-cost items like books, off-the-shelf software and consumer electronics. But there may be non-core aspects of your business where you can experiment with e-commerce. A successful effort will not only generate sales dollars at the margin, it will help drive greater traffic to your site, which contributes indirectly to revenue growth.

So, the moral of the story is, if you don't have a Web site already, invest in one. If you have one, take a fresh look at it and consider how you could improve its design, the amount of information on it, how frequently that information is updated, and how well linked it is to other sites. The following discussion focuses on specific aspects of your site where you can get the greatest bang for the buck.

Writing, Design and Hosting

This section is for companies that don't yet have a Web site, or that have one designed by a friend of the receptionist's teenage son as a school project. How do you go about producing something professional that will make a good impression?

Don't fall for the "so easy you can do it yourself" come-on of the commercial Web packages. Home-made Web sites almost always look that, and that's a waste of money when your site can make you look like a much bigger and more impressive company for very little money.

You have two basic choices: to hire a professional copywriter and a designer with Web experience; or to hire a one-stop Web site development firm. The first choice will cost you less — if you have experience managing copywriters and designers. If you don't, you'll find the process frustrating. You probably won't understand what the creative people need from you, and they won't understand why you're not happy with their work. Like many specialists, advertising creative people require experienced care and feeding to produce good results.

The one-stop Web firm will have people on its staff who function as account executives. Theoretically, they know how to get the information from you that the creatives need. They also know how to present you with options in a way you can understand and can guide you to make the right decisions. They can then translate all this into something the creatives understand. Naturally, this costs more than managing everything yourself.

What *will* it cost you? That's a short question with a long answer. If you're managing the copywriter and designer yourself, and producing a fairly simple site with a few dozen pages, you can expect to spend as little as $2,500. That gets you a set of files that your designer can upload to a server where your registered domain name resides. (Registering a Web domain is one of the great bargains of the century. If nobody else is using it, you can gain exclusive use of a domain name for $75 a year.) This may be on your own network — which requires technical expertise and appropriate software. But these days, you can get a commercial hosting account with one of the big providers for between $15 and $50 per month. If you don't already have technical systems and staff to host it yourself, it won't pay you to acquire it.

Keeping that simple site up-to-date requires you to buy time periodically from the creative guys, but you can typically revise several pages for only a few hundred dollars. Do that six times a year and pay your $50 hosting bill each month, and you're spending less than $2,000 a year. That's what makes the Web such a B2B marketing bargain!

If you're going the one-stop shop route, you will probably be presented with two choices. Most of the vendors we have dealt with have tried to sell us on a "dynamic" site design, instead of a "static" design. "Static" means the good old-fashioned approach of designing a set of pages in the Web's basic HTML programming language, beginning with a home page and branching out to various sub-pages, like this:

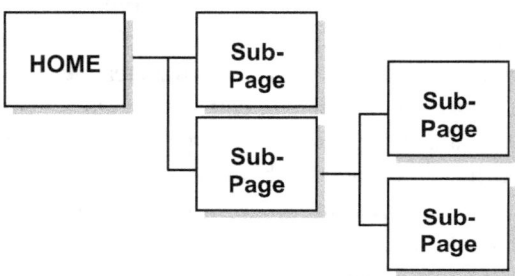

Hyperlinks on the pages, plus a set of navigation buttons, allows users to move around the site at will.

A "dynamic" site stores all of its content in a database and actually composes HTML pages on the fly when a user requests that page. Pretty cool, huh? Also pretty expensive. At a one-stop shop, you might pay $5,000 - $10,000 for a static Web site, but the starting price for a dynamic site will be $20,000-30,000, and they frequently run into the hundreds of thousands of dollars.

Why would anybody want one? When a site gets very large — hundreds or thousands of pages — or is an e-commerce site involving a lot of transactions, a dynamic design makes it far easier and cheaper to maintain. Let's say you want to change the name of a product or service. With a static site, somebody would have to check every page to find references to that product or service and change them individually. With a dynamic site, you change the one data element representing that product or service, and it is automatically updated every time a page is composed by the system.

We warned you that the answer would be a long one. The bottom line is that, for most B2B businesses, a static Web site design will be entirely adequate and will save you a lot of money. But if you know going in that your site will be very large or involve substantial e-commerce, you'll be better off paying the higher fare for a dynamic site.

Getting People to Visit

A Web site is like a retail store: it doesn't reach out and communicate for you. You have to entice people to enter.

A growing stream of magazine articles, books, Web sites and newsletters are devoted to the complex business of making yourself visible on the World Wide Web. So we'll restrict ourselves to some basics to get your started.

1. **Content.** Like every other aspect of marketing, the content of your Web site has to be about your customers, not about you. In thinking about what you will put on a Web site, go beyond your sales pitch. Sure, there's a place for that, but the Web also allows you to *do* things for visitors. Give them free advice (which contributes to their buying decision, of course). Invite their input. Direct them to other information available on the Web. Provide samples of your products, if feasible. Basically, think about everything you might do in a one-to-one selling effort, and try to come up with ways to do it online. This won't attract people to your site in the first place, but it may get them to come back.

There's also a technical side to site content. The most popular online search engines (more about them below) actually analyze the text content of your site and use this information to create their listings. To have your site come up more often in Web searches, you need to think about the words and phrases that somebody might use to find you. In writing the content of the site, you need to make sure that these words and phrases appear regularly, so the search engines will find them. Let's say one of your key phrases is "document storage" and that you really want people interested in document storage to find three particular pages on your site. On those three pages, the phrase "document storage" needs to make up between 2% and 5% of the text; if the page runs 200 words, you would want to use the phrase between four and ten times. Strange, eh? It also runs counter to a basic rule of good writing, which is not to repeat things too much. But it's good to keep in mind as you edit the text of your site.

2.   **Site Structure.** A few years ago, the rage in Web design was the "frames-based" site. Instead of giving the visitor a single page, the site would actually display multiple pages in "frames." Typically there would be a "header frame" at the top, a "navigation frame" on the left, and the main "content frame" on the right. It was cool, and also made getting around the site easier for users. But frames are fast disappearing from Web design, because it turns out that search engines can't handle them. When a search engine hits a frames-based site, it "sees" only the first page of the site and ignores everything else. So make sure your design is "frameless" going in.

3.   **Registration with Search Engines.** Once your site is finished, you need to register it with the major search engines. This will put your Web domain on a list, and the next time the search engine does one of its global searches of content on the World Wide Web, it will check your site as well. Presto, listings for your site will begin appearing when users do a search on the right words. You can do all the registration work yourself — there's an excellent Web site, www.searchenginewatch.com, with instructions, or do a Web search on "search engine" to find other resources. Or you can use one of the countless services available on the Web to do it for you at a cost of a few hundred dollars. But either way, don't omit this step, or your site will be stuck in a dark and musty corner of the World Wide Web.

4.   **Links From Other Sites.** Getting listed on the search engines is one thing. Having your site come up within

the first 20 or 30 listings is another. You probably already receive email messages from companies that promise to get you in the top 10. They may or may not be able to help you. You can also pay the major sites to list you favorably. But unless the Web is central to what you do — because you sell software online, let's say — that's an expense you can avoid. Instead, spend time getting your Web site listed in online directories of your industry, on the sites of trade associations you belong to, and anywhere else you can think of. The biggest search engines rate the importance of your site based partly on how many other Web sites have links that point to it. The more sites that point to you, the more valuable your site is considered, and the more frequently it will appear in search results.

5. **Promotion.** Finally, just like a store, your Web site needs promotion to attract visitors. Everything you do in advertising, public relations and direct marketing should include your Web address. If you do email marketing, include in your email multiple links to different parts of your site. One of the best ways to build site traffic is to publish a newsletter as a page on your site, and send out email broadcasts that announce each issue, with links back to that page. Of course, the newsletter has to be interesting and worthwhile in its own right for this approach to work.

We've tried to give you a taste here of a very full menu of ideas and issues. But that's the way it is in marketing and sales. The Web may have created wonderful B2B marketing opportunities. But the down side is that the B2B marketer has to become familiar with another specialized body of knowledge in order to take advantage of those opportunities.

CHAPTER 11

Sales Support

Sales support, huh? Brochures and stuff. Boring!

If this is what you're thinking — you're right. For the most part, sales support ain't the sexiest part of marketing. And in this chapter, we're not going to talk about the terrifically cool things that B2B companies sometimes do for sales support. Trade show booths with video walls, rotating displays and leggy blondes or guys with killer abs. Multimedia road shows with computer animation, interactive displays and professional actors as presenters. Inflatable King Kong dolls mounted on the side of the Empire State Building. It's all good fun and, in the right circumstances, can be effective. But day in, day out, good marketing is a matter of blocking and tackling. Even relatively unsophisticated B2B marketers often do the flashy stuff well because it is so new and exciting that they pay it close attention. The investment will be utterly wasted, however, if you fail at the day-to-day business of finding prospects and selling to them.

And to do that job well, your salespeople need sales support materials and activities. You want them to achieve as much as possible in the shortest amount of time, and that's what sales support is designed to do. The trick is to spend the right amount of money on the right stuff.

The Brochure

Before the age of PowerPoint and the Internet, B2B companies typically invested a lot of money in producing pieces of paper: brochures, price lists, sales sheets, article reprints, and so on. One of the ways in which the Internet saves you money as a marketer is by allowing you to provide most of that information through your Web site. On the Web, you can revise and update as often as you want at a tiny fraction of printing costs.

But no matter how cool the Internet may be, your salespeople need a brochure. Why? Because they run into a lot of prospective customers who say, "I can't meet with you right now. Can you send me something?" To continue the dialog, they have to have something to send. And at the end of a sales meeting, they need to leave something behind that will help their new contact introduce your company to people up the ladder.

Producing brochures has a tendency to turn into a fiscal black hole. Why? Because your business keeps changing, and the brochure has to keep up with the changes. Whenever you introduce something new, you need a new brochure for it, don't you? The result is that you are constantly redesigning and printing, storing and throwing away out-of-date copies.

You can keep brochure costs to a minimum by using a 9x12 presentation folder. It may be as simple as a four-page piece with an inside pocket — giving you room for your marketing message on the front cover and inside front cover — or it may have multiple inside pages. The reason we like it is that inside pocket. That's where you put loose 8.5 x 11 pages that you create with word-processing and print in your office. (We usually recommend creating a special letterhead for these pages that matches your brochure, because it gives a professional look at low cost.) With this format, you keep the presentation folder very generic: your name and logo, and a general introduction to your company. All the detailed information, which is likely to change frequently, goes on the loose pages. That way, you can afford to pay for a professional and impressive folder, because you will only be printing it every 3-4 years. Meanwhile, you can change the information on the loose pages as often as you want, because you are printing them "just in time." You can even email the individual pages to people who ask you to "send them something."

What should you expect to pay? It varies with how "hot" you want the design to be, how many colors you will print it in, and how many you want. A full-color folder with a Fortune 500 look, in a quantity of 6,000-10,000, may cost you $20,000 - 30,000. A couple of thousand black-and-white or 2-color folders will cost you $4,000 – $6,000. You can certainly spend less, but if the result looks cheap or amateurish, you might as well not have spent the money at all.

The PowerPoint Presentation

PowerPoint was a breakthrough product that allowed non-designers to create a customized presentation on slides, a PC screen or printed pages. And it's still powerful today. It doesn't have the sizzle of a nice brochure, but it can be revised quickly and easily, without spending a dime. Because of its "bullet-point" structure, it boils down your sales message to the key essentials. Since it's a digital file, your salespeople can email it to prospects and take them through it on the phone when a face-to-face meeting isn't possible.

Here are a few guidelines for effective presentations:

- **Have a design professional set up a template for you, including background art and the layout of bulleted text.** Make sure that the designer follows whatever graphic standards you already have in place, such as the look and feel of your brochure. The appearance of all your presentations will communicate a professional image and a consistent brand identity. And frankly, we've all seen the standard Microsoft layouts once too often.

- **Create standard pages with your company description and other basic information.** Like the master page design, this makes sure your sales-people communicate the official story of your company, not their own private impressions.

- **Provide your salespeople with a template file with the master design and standard pages**, and let them create their own presentations. If essential information about your company changes, you will have to update the template and make sure your salespeople are using the latest information.

Do's and Don'ts

We have seen a lot of sales support activity over the years, and there are some major do's and don'ts you should keep in mind:

- **Do keep your sales support materials up-to-date.** In earlier chapters, we advised you to review your value proposition and targeting regularly. One of the follow-up steps should be to revise your sales materials — and that's where our favorite brochure format will save you lots of money.

- **Do put someone in charge of graphic standards.** Good marketers make sure that the look and feel of all their marketing materials is consistent. Why? Because it creates the very desirable impression that your company speaks with a single voice, not a multitude of conflicting voices. But when sales support materials get a lot of use, people tend to start changing things, and your standard look and feel rapidly disintegrates. At a minimum, graphic standards should cover the color and placement of your logo and company name and the colors and typefaces used in your materials.

- **Don't ever, under any circumstances, use your sales support materials for direct marketing.** In other words, don't mail your brochure, with a business card stapled to the front, to 5,000 people. You'd be better off setting fire to them — at least it would keep you warm. First of all, your brochure is too expensive to distribute widely and blindly. Second, it does not have an appropriate DM format, does not make a simple and exciting offer, does not in fact have any of the characteristics of effective direct marketing. So why on earth would you put it in an envelope and send it to people you don't know? Only because you haven't thought of something better to do.

Other Stuff

These are basics. The rest of your advertising and marketing program can provide additional materials: reprints of articles that mention your company (generated by PR), white papers and case studies, and copies of ads that you placed in trade show issues of magazines.

Trade shows are another basic, but there's not much we can add to your understanding. You pay a specialty company to sell you a standard booth with custom graphics, or you spend a pile of money on a custom booth. You set it up, staff it with salespeople, and do the old meet-and-greet. It's basically a sales environment, but trade shows are also great places to introduce new products or services because so many potential customers and the business press are sure to be there.

If you're in a technology business, you may be able to equip your salespeople with demos that run on their laptops. If the sales process involves estimating from a lengthy list of established prices and costs, you can have a programmer develop an estimating system in Excel. This will let salespeople provide price quotes on the spot. Anything that will help salespeople identify genuine prospects and close deals in less time is well worth your investment.

B2B
Sales

CHAPTER 12

Selling By the Numbers

As we noted in the introduction to this book, the B2B world is full of people who must manage sales professionals without being one. It also contains many good intuitive salespeople, like natural athletes, who find it difficult to manage others because they don't truly understand *how* they do what they do.

The rest of this book is for them, and for anyone who needs to better understand selling as a business process that can be managed and improved. There are mysteries in selling — but they have to do with the intangibles of the human spirit. How salespeople thrive in a career that involves large daily doses of rejection. How they find enjoyment in something that causes most people anxiety and embarrassment. Exactly how they connect with strangers, create relationships, find points of leverage and drive to the close in an intricate dance of seduction. All that is the mystery. But the process of B2B selling? That's a matter of knowing what you're doing and doing it by the numbers.

The Lebsack Curve

But let's start our discussion with a fundamental question. Do you really need salespeople? If so, why?

A surprisingly large number of B2B businesses do not have anybody on staff with the word "sales" in their title. We even know entrepreneur-founders who are proud of the fact that they don't have salespeople on the team. They have project managers. They have regional directors. They have vice presidents of business development. In most cases, these people wear two hats. They are supposed to sell new business but also to service that business. They find the prospect, write the proposal, then manage the actual work or product delivery before going on to the next piece of business.

We worked for several years with a Swiss-owned company that provided utilities and construction companies with industrial testing. They inspected welding and x-rayed pipes. They slump-tested wet concrete and smashed dry concrete cylinders to test their strength.

One of their division managers complained to us that he felt stuck in terms of growing the revenues of his group. He said, "We bid a lot of work and win our share. We work those projects and do a great job. And when they're done, we look around and panic, because there's no new business. So we start hunting for jobs and bidding like mad. We win some and get to work. But we never get anywhere. The revenues go up and down like a yo-yo."

Or like the curve of a wave. The wave goes up and the wave goes down, and the boat floating in the water does not move forward an inch.

In honor of this division manager, we named his problem "The Lebsack Curve." It describes exactly why every B2B company must have employees whose top responsibility is hunting for new business. If everybody in your company is responsible for *doing* the work and nobody is primarily responsible for *finding* the work, you are on the Lebsack Curve. Your business is stuck riding the revenue wave up and down without any forward progress. In a hot market, your revenues will certainly go up and you can become a sales hero just by answering the phone. But that's not selling. That's minding the store. Scooping ice cream during a heat wave. Retailing umbrellas when it's raining.

Selling is a proactive business process. It's a hunt for business in which you seek to control as many elements of the process as possible, because it gives you some hope of controlling your company's destiny. If you're just waiting for the phone to ring while you're working on something else, the marketplace is in the driver's seat. In good times, you'll prosper. In bad times, you'll be road kill.

Challenges of the B2B Sale

The proactive B2B sale offers unique challenges and demands different techniques from the typical B2C sale. Let's go back a minute to the principles we noted at the start of our discussion of B2B marketing.

In Chapter 6, we noted that most B2B markets are small, consisting of fewer than five thousand buyers worldwide. In such niche markets, buyers at different companies tend to know each other. They gossip. When a vendor has good solutions, word gets around. When a vendor stinks, word gets around about that, too. This is important in understanding the difference between how B2B companies typically sell — and how they should be selling.

What's the most popular form of selling activity among B2B companies? By a wide margin, it's coldcalling: getting on the phone with total strangers and trying to sell them something. The average conversion rate for coldcalling — meaning the success rate at turning a telephone call into a sales meeting — is about 4%, meaning 4 meetings for every 100 calls made.

If you get the feeling there's something wrong with this picture, you're correct. Though some of it is necessary, coldcalling is a bad match for most B2B markets. It treats a small, community-like B2B marketplace as though it were a big, anonymous B2C marketplace. It fails to leverage the natural intimacy of the market to achieve success.

It is much more powerful to base selling on relationships and referrals. If a potential buyer has been referred to your company, or you are calling on a customer who has bought from you in the past, the conversion rate to a meeting is in the 30-50% range. That's an average of 2-4 calls in order to get one meeting. So, being proactive does not mean knocking on a thousand anonymous doors. It means carefully working the relationships you have in order to produce more. Asking for referrals. Going to the conventions your customers attend and trolling for introductions. Being a speaker on a conference panel. Compiling the contacts, finding ways to stay in touch with them, creating opportunities for relationship-building.

More Challenges

In Chapter 6, we also noted that, in B2B, your prospective customers are not lone amateurs doing the work of purchasing in their spare time. You're facing buyers, or often a committee of buyers, who are being paid to make the right choice, and whose careers may depend on the choice they make.

For this reason, the typical B2B sale is a long cycle requiring days, weeks or months. The high-pressure, "always-be-closing" techniques that can succeed in B2C are counter-productive in the B2B sale. Buyers need to take their time, because the stakes are high. And because the B2B sale has a long cycle, it requires a sales management system that measures and motivates every step of the way.

What does this mean? Salespeople are typically evaluated on that most basic measure: sales volume. Their compensation is based in whole or in part on how many dollars in sales they generate in a given period. So it's natural to measure their performance in the same way. But the long-cycle B2B sales makes that measurement problematic when it comes to predicting how successful a salesperson will be.

Here's an example. Say you hire a new salesperson. You assign her a territory and put her on a mix of salary and commission. You set the expectation that, within 6 months, she will close her first sale with a value of $50,000, and that within her first 12 months, she will close sales worth $250,000, rising to $1 million over the succeeding 12 months. Then you sit back and wait for the results.

Six months later, she's obviously working hard but has booked no business. Nine months later, she has managed to close only $20,000. Things aren't working out, which is unfortunate for both of you. But much, much worse — it took nine months for you both to find out. Nine months is a long time in business. This only has to happen a couple of times for the growth of your business to be set back. And your employee has probably been laboring in isolation, growing increasingly desperate, not sure what she is doing wrong and unable to change her performance.

Is there a better way? You bet there is. There's no reason to wait nine months to know what's going on. You should be able to get your first read within 30 days, and then identify specific problems and help that salesperson improve her performance. The secret is to break down the selling process into its stages, set milestones for each one, and measure performance against those milestones. That gives you the information you need to manage the process rather than being slave to the results. It's the means for both you and your sales staff to take destiny into your own hands to the greatest possible extent. In the next chapters, we'll lay out the stages in detail, and then explain how to measure what's going on.

CHAPTER 13

Stages of the Sale

It's a big marketplace out there, with people in all stages of readiness to buy. Excuse us if we get pedantic for a moment and explain a classification system for the stages of the B2B sale, formulated by Robert Rogus, a Practice Leader with our firm who in a 30-year career has created and led corporate sales teams responsible for hundreds of millions of dollars of revenue growth.

In the long-cycle B2B sale, our system defines four buyer classifications, and three stages that connect them:

Classification	Stage
Contact	
⇩	Appointment
Suspect	⇩
⇩	Proposal
Prospect	⇩
⇩	Close
Customer	⇩

Contacts

"Contacts" are people that you know exist — but about which you know precious little else. They may be people who filled out a "bingo card" in an industry magazine requesting information about your company. They may be visitors to your Web site or names on a direct response list or on business cards left at your trade show booth. All you know about them is a name, job title, company and a telephone or email address, if you're lucky enough to know even that. And you know that, because they inquired or because their company and job title fits your marketing target (see Chapter 3), there is at least the possibility that this person may do business with you.

With Contacts, your goal is to schedule an Appointment, preferably face-to-face but at least by telephone or videoconference in order to conduct a Needs Analysis. (More about this later.) The Appointment is the crucial step in which you will learn enough to decide whether or not to invest more time in this person.

Suspects

If you get through the Contact and Needs Analysis and you still think there is opportunity there, your Contact is upgraded to a Suspect. Suspects are people or organizations that appear to have a need you can fulfill, and who have, or soon will, request a proposal or price from you. Based on your Appointment, your blank slate has now been filled in with a lot of specific information, and you have an opportunity to take action by writing a proposal and/or quoting a price.

Prospects

You have a Prospect on your hands when—

- You submit your proposal or price and do not get an immediate rejection
- You can either assume or determine that the organization has the ability to pay you
- There is an accepted timetable for reaching a decision

As you can see from that list of criteria, a Prospect has a high likelihood of turning into an actual sale. Once Suspects turn into Prospects, you can and should focus as much time and resource on them as you can, because they will justify it over the long term.

And a Customer is — well, you don't really need us to explain it, do you? It's that pleasant "ca-ching" sound you hear in the back of your mind when somebody on the other side of the table says "Yes."

Why The Definitions Matter

Why are we being so picky in our definitions? There are a couple of reasons.

First, the key to "unsuccess" in sales is to devote precious hours to pursuing business from companies that don't deserve your attention. It's far, far better to quickly disqualify the low-potential Contacts you meet than to waste time trying to sell them. Each stage of our process involves weeding out those who don't make the cut. Emotionally, it's hard to let go of the complete goat, but your time is the most important resource you have and wasting it is your shortest road to failure. The only way you can make the right choices is to have very clear and firm definitions in mind.

Second, precisely defining the components of the sales process is what lets you measure progress in the early stages, when there is still time to correct problems.

In the next chapters, we'll go into more detail about the stages themselves and the means for using them to measure performance.

CHAPTER 14

The Appointment, Part 1

Most sales first start to become a sale through an initial meeting, whether it takes place face-to-face, through a teleconference, or even a videoconference. A face-to-face meeting is always preferable; it just gets hard to do when your business is conducted across borders and time zones.

Let's Not Talk About Me, Darling

Every sales professional wants to get in front of the Contact and turn him or her into a Suspect. But remarkably few people understand how to get the most out of that first Appointment. Why do we say that? Because most salespeople start their appointment by describing their company and talking about its products and services. In other words, by talking about themselves.

Bad idea.

When you meet a total stranger, and that stranger does all the talking, and the talk is all about how great he or she is — what's your reaction? Exactly. You can't wait for the conversation to end. On the other hand, the single most powerful way to make a positive impression is to listen very, very carefully to what the other person says, and then say something intelligent in response. That's what's called active listening, and it is amazingly effective. That's why the most successful salespeople do a lot more listening than talking during the Appointment. Not only do they make a better impression, they are actually putting themselves in the strongest possible position to win the business.

Why? When they finally do get to the point of talking about their products or services, they do it from an understanding of the contact's needs, wants and fears. This allows them to shape their message — talking about products or services that meet the need, supply the want or ease the fear. There is no stronger position from which to sell. Instead of throwing darts in the dark, they see their target clearly and have the best possible chance to hit it.

Opening Up

It is not always easy to get potential buyers to talk about themselves. Some are naturally uncommunicative. Others are too harried to think straight. But many encourage the salesperson to talk as a form of defense: it keeps knowledge, and therefore power, in their own hands. The salesperson's job is to establish enough trust to make the buyer open up. The way to do this is by demonstrating a bit of knowledge about the buyer's company, and then asking questions.

We're amazed at the number of salespeople who still come in our door with absolutely no knowledge of what our company does. This is the Internet Age, for crying out loud! Five minutes spent at our Web site will give them enough to open the meeting with a couple of intelligent comments. Having demonstrated a glancing knowledge, they will have earned the right to ask for more information. Without that knowledge, they have to work a lot harder to earn our respect.

Questions, Questions

Once you have earned the right to ask questions, what questions do you ask?

The standard advice is to ask "open-ended" questions — ones that can't be answered with a simple yes or no. Good idea. It will be a real short conversation if all the buyer says is "Yep" or "Nope." Inexperienced salespeople are also advised to gather as much information about the company as they can. So they ask things like "What equipment are you using?" and "How long have you had it?" All good stuff — but not very effective when it comes to uncovering the buyer's real needs.

For the following discussion, we are indebted to Neil Rackham, a researcher and consultant who has focused on the face-to-face, big-ticket sale and is the author of *SPIN Selling* and over 50 articles on the topic. Rackham has created an excellent framework for understanding the different kinds of questions that salespeople need to ask, and done quantitative research to identify which are most effective. We will use Rackham's framework to explain the results we have observed in our decades of B2B sales and marketing consultation.

Scoping the Situation

The easiest questions to ask are those that explore the situation. These are the "What equipment are you using?" kind of questions, which gather basic factual information that help you assess the possibility that the buyer will buy from you. If you're selling widgets, you need to find out if this person is a consumer of widgets, when the last widget purchase was made, what the purchasing process for widgets is, and so forth.

What Rackham's research revealed, however, was that inexperienced salespeople ask a lot more situation questions than they should. Specifically, his data showed that asking a lot of situation questions tends to lead to a failed sales call. Not that the information isn't useful. It's just that situation questions will never uncover real needs that the buyer feels an urgency about meeting. Need and urgency are the raw materials of a sale.

More powerful than situation questions are ones that identify problems: "What kind of difficulties do you have at peak periods with your current widget?" "Is your current widget reliable enough, or do you have a lot of downtime with it?" "Are you having problems with on-time delivery?" These are powerful for two reasons. First, they tend to uncover information you can use: a problem you may be able to solve for the buyer. Second, they are more interesting to the buyer than a recitation of facts about his or her business. Problems are what make the buyer wake up at three in the morning in a cold sweat. And Rackham's research confirmed that successful sales calls contained many more problem questions than situation questions.

Drilling Down

So far, so good. Even people with no training in sales usually find their way to asking problem and situation questions. But effective salespeople find ways to drill deeper — to uncover the factors that create an urgency to solve the problem.

Rackham's research showed that successful salespeople move on from asking about problems to "implication questions." These probe for the meaning of the problems that are revealed by the problem questions. Let's say one of your problem questions revealed that a buyer is not quite happy with the degree of downtime on his widget. Not a major complaint, but a point you might be able to use. An implication question would try to pinpoint the cost to the buyer of this problem, like so:

> *Buyer:* Our only problem is restarts. The widget locks up every few days and has to be restarted. It's a pain.
>
> *Seller:* What impact is that having on your operation?
>
> *Buyer:* Not much. It's mostly an annoyance.
>
> *Seller:* Have you ever lost data because it?
>
> *Buyer:* Actually, we have. That's why we put in a remote backup system that backs up everything at night.
>
> *Seller:* And what does that cost you?

Buyer: It was about five grand to set up and a few hundred a month for the service.

Seller: How about the productivity of your people? Do they lose work time when it locks up? How much time do they spend hanging around waiting for the restart?

Buyer: Not much, really. Fifteen minutes, maybe a half-hour at the most between the time that performance first degrades and we have to reboot.

Seller: You mentioned that the widget locks up every few days. That means between eight and twelve restarts a month, right?

Buyer: I didn't think it was that many, but maybe —

Seller: If each restart puts an employee on hold for a half hour, that means you're losing up to six hours a month for each employee who accesses the widget.

Buyer: Jeez, you're right. I never did the math on that. We've got ten people on the system, and we could be wasting six hours a month on each one?

Seller: Plus the money you're spending on the remote backup system. If your people are clerical to mid-level staff, you're probably spending $15-25 per hour per employee. So your lost time could be costing you up to $1,500 each month.

Not all products and services lend themselves to such a clear analysis of the cost of problems. For many, it is more a matter of missed opportunities or the risks of a much larger cost. But the principle is the same. Implication questions don't stop at getting the buyer to state a problem — they explore what the problem really means for the buyer. You can see the potential power of this approach to turn what the buyer perceives as a low-level annoyance into a problem that requires a solution.

Creating a Solution

The last kind of question defined by Rackham involves your proposed solution to the buyer's problem. This is where you finally get to talk about what your company can do. But instead of throwing your capabilities up on the wall and hoping that something sticks, solution questions turn the buyer's attention from understanding the problem to solving it. Picking up on our imaginary conversation from the previous section...

> *Seller:* If you had a widget that didn't lock up so often, would it help?
>
> *Buyer:* Sounds like it. If these numbers are real. I'd have to look into it.
>
> *Seller:* Let's stay you had a widget that was so fault-tolerant it would run continuously for six months before needing a restart. It seems like that could save you 360 hours in lost staff time, worth up to $9,000. Over a year, it's $18,000. You'd also be able to go back to your weekly tape backup system instead of paying for the remote service.
>
> *Buyer:* That could make a real difference to us.
>
> *Seller:* Well, let me show you something that *will* make that difference. It's our MaxiWidget 6000...

The solution question is your chance to state, or get the buyer to state for you, the *value* your solution provides. It sets the stage for you to describe the particular offering of your company that will solve the problem and deliver that value. Finally, you get to do what most salespeople do, wrongly, at the beginning of the Appointment — tell the buyer all about how great your products and services really are.

But the most important benefit of this approach is not a matter of preparing the buyer to hear your pitch. It is in setting the context for the buyer's decision-making.

In the case above, if Seller had started talking at the beginning of the Appointment about his great widget that runs for six months with no downtime and only costs $7,000, Buyer would have experienced a bad case of sticker shock. Seven grand to eliminate a minor annoyance? Forget about it! But if Buyer is convinced that she has an $18,000+ problem on her hands, it's a completely different decision. Buyer may still decide that the company has to limp along with its old widget, but at least the new widget is being considered in the context of its true value.

CHAPTER 15

The Appointment, Part 2

Do you watch those home repair or woodworking shows on TV? Once upon a time, there was only PBS's *This Old House*, but in the 200+ channel universe of cable TV, there are now dozens of programs with earnest people showing you how build cabinets, fix windows and restore Victorian gazebos.

They all have one thing in common. The people on the shows never make a mistake. Ever. Which is a real shame. Because the one thing that most of us want to know is how to make those two boards fit together even though we cut them to the wrong size, or what to do after we have snapped off the fitting we were supposed to gently ease off the pipe

Selling is like that, too. The imaginary conversations between Buyer and Seller in the last chapter make it look easy. Well, it's not. The following are tips to guide you as you try to introduce these techniques into your own selling efforts.

Conversation, Not Inquisition

First, the conversation that takes place during your Appointment is just that — a conversation, not an inquisition. No potential buyer will sit still for a long list of questions or wait for you to check off boxes on a questionnaire. The conversation is most powerful if it is based on a mutual interest in solving problems. You are trying to give the potential buyer an opportunity to stop and think about his or her needs and how well they are being met. It may even be the only chance the buyer has had to stop and think in a long time.

One Skill at a Time

Second, if you're going to try this, we urge you to practice one skill at a time. This is not easy stuff, and it takes a lot of practice to get it right. So make a resolution in your next appointment to ask problem questions as well as situation questions. See if that reveals more potential opportunities. Try that for a few sales calls until you have a gut feel for how to transition from asking about the situation to probing for problems. When you feel pretty good about that, it's time to try implication questions. And so on.

Quantity, Not Quality

Another trick to mastering new skills is to practice them a lot. We all tend to be too hard on ourselves when learning a new skill. We want to stop and work each little component until it's perfect. But research makes it absolutely clear that the fastest way to learn something is to practice it a lot without worrying about how well you're doing. Just do it, notice the mistakes, but don't beat yourself up about them. As counterintuitive as it may seem, the kinder you are to yourself, the faster you become proficient.

Advance Planning

There is one area, however, where some attention to detail, in advance, will pay off. It's with implication questions. The plain fact is that very few of us are smart enough to come up with implication questions on the fly. In order to see through to the implication of problems, you need to go into the Appointment with some knowledge of what the company does, what kind of problems it may have, and what the implication of those problems is likely to be. As you gain experience in asking about problems, you will see patterns emerge. Certain problems will arise over and over again, and they will have predictable impacts on the buyer's business. So in preparation for the appointment, it helps to jot down some likely implication questions that could apply to the kind of company you are about to visit.

Plan B

Finally, there is always the possibility that you ask all the right questions in all the right ways and get absolutely zilch. The person on the other side of the desk isn't going to work with you. You can't figure out why he or she agreed to see you in the first place.

Our favorite story about this concerns a client who sold software that processes author royalties to publishing companies. Royalties are a nightmare to calculate, because the publishing industry has lots of bizarre practices and book contracts are idiosyncratic things.

Our client made a sales call on a publisher who started the Appointment by explaining that his company had no problems with its royalty processing. Royalty statements and payments were issued on time. They were accurate and complete. The authors were happy. The accountants were happy. Our hero asked the obvious question: "Why am I here?"

The publisher fixed him with a beady stare and said, "She's retiring."

Now there's a problem that doesn't need any implication questions to reveal itself! So our client got the sale.

But there are Appointments where you can't open the oyster no matter how hard you try. In that case, go to Plan B. Make sure you get across a few basic points about what your company does, and ask for a referral to another company. Then get the heck out of there so that you can spend time with somebody more useful.

Subjective Factors

Our discussion so far has focused on the rational parts of the buying decision. Problems. Solutions. Cost versus benefit. But we all know that irrational factors figure large in the sales process. For every objective reason to buy (or not to buy), there is a subjective reason based on the buyer's experience. You will not be able to uncover every dark secret in one meeting. But during the Appointment, you can ask a few questions that reveal attitudes that may be critical to the success of this sale. Perhaps the buyer has had a bad experience with vendors in your industry, and is skeptical about your claims. Maybe you bear a striking resemblance to the buyer's long-lost son. Perhaps the buyer feels insecure about his or her job, and wants to avoid taking risks. Or the buyer's brother-in-law may happen to work for the company's current vendor.

During the wrap-up (see below), here are a few questions that you may want to work in:

- "When you have bought [your products or services] before, what have vendors done that you really liked? What has a vendor done to annoy you?"

- "From what I read, your industry is undergoing [whatever it is]. How is that affecting your company?"

- "These are challenging times for everyone. How is your company coping with [whatever the economic conditions are]?"

The answers to these questions can tell you what to emphasize in your proposal, quote or next meeting. A subjective or emotional issue is often far more powerful in the business decision than a dozen objective reasons. And it pays to put that power on your side whenever you can.

Wrapping up

Your next sales call may not turn out as well as Seller's sales call. It may leave you wanting to put your fist through the nearest wall instead. But however it goes, if you have done your job right, you will know one of three things:

- You can upgrade your Contact into a Suspect. You have uncovered needs you can satisfy and generated a sense of urgency about meeting them.
- There's a need, but your implication questions did not motivate the Contact to consider it a problem needing a solution.
- You have largely wasted the past 30-40 minutes on somebody who won't buy.

If it's the first option, then you need to do two things. First, you need to identify the players. Is the person you're meeting the only decision-maker? Who else is involved in the purchasing decision? The other thing you need to know about is your competition. Is the buyer looking at solutions from other companies at this point? If so, which ones?

Second, you need to get permission for the next step. This is best done by summing up the problem and solution revealed by your questions, something like this:

Seller: So, downtime with your widget may be a real problem costing you $18,000 or more a year in lost productivity. You're also unhappy with its operating speed, and I'd have to agree that you're not getting the performance you deserve. My suggestion is that you look at replacing it with our widget. With less downtime and faster performance, it should give you payback in six months or less. Can I give you a proposal on that so you can evaluate the savings? Or is there some other step we should take?

If it's the second or third options, then you are better off not spending time on a proposal. Sum up with (mostly) the truth: that there doesn't seem to be a fit at the moment between the suspect's needs and your products or services but that there may be at some point in the future. Be gracious and grateful for the suspect's time. Then you can leave. If the Appointment uncovered a need but little urgency about action, keep the Contact on the list to receive newsletters and other marketing materials, and schedule follow-up in three to six months. If the meeting was a complete waste of time, however, you are better of consigning the Contact to the circular file.

CHAPTER 16

From Suspect to Prospect

Whatever the outcome of your Appointment, you should be able to leave it with a well-earned sense of accomplishment. You either found a Suspect with a near-term need, a Suspect with needs who may buy in the future, or a complete goat you can take off your list forever. Anyway you slice it, you win. You've got a near-term opportunity, a long-term opportunity, or you have avoided wasting time on presenting solutions to a company that will never buy from you.

Making Progress

If your Appointment uncovered a Suspect with a near-term need, there could be any one of several next steps. Maybe the Suspect wants a "ballpark" quote to assess the cost of doing business with you. Perhaps the Suspect is willing to review a full-blown proposal, or to add you to the list for a soon-to-be-released Request For Proposal (RFP). One great way to improve your odds of success, by the way, is to ask how the RFP is coming together and see if the buyer would like any advice on it, based on your experience. If the buyer welcomes your comments, it creates an opportunity to influence the RFP in ways that benefit your company. All too often, RFPs take a commodity-based approach and provide no opportunity for you to sell value. Influencing the writing of the RFP can avoid that trap.

On the other hand, the best you may be able to do is to schedule another meeting.

In some of these cases, it is clear that you are making progress toward a sale. In others, it's not so clear. If the Suspect invited you to another meeting, are you moving forward or being offered a trip down a blind alley?

The larger the value of the sale, the harder it is to tell. According to Neil Rackham's research, in major-account sales, fewer than 10% of initial sales calls result in a clear "sale or no sale" outcome. So you have to evaluate progress using different criteria.

The key, in our experience, is to see movement toward a decision on the Suspect's part. This may be an agreement to visit your office and see a demonstration. Maybe the next scheduled meeting is with executives farther up the ladder. Or the company agrees to a trial with your product or service. These are all signs of progress toward an eventual sale. Another meeting with the same buyer to cover the same ground is not.

Becoming a Prospect

Through any and all of these actions, you are trying to turn a Suspect into a Prospect. A Prospect, remember, is a company that has all of the characteristics of a Suspect, plus three vital signs:

- The ability to actually pay for your solution
- A positive response to — or at least not an immediate rejection of — your price
- A willingness to set a timetable for making the purchase decision

Credit Check

In our fast-changing economy and fast-globalizing world, more and more B2B companies are facing an issue that only the multinationals used to confront. The issue is: how do I know if I'll get paid?

If you're selling to one of the Fortune 1000 in the US, you probably worry more about bureaucratic barriers to getting paid than about the company's ability to pay. For smaller customers in the US, Dun & Bradstreet and other companies can at least give you some insight into the company's credit history and financials. But when you're dealing with companies overseas, as we increasingly do, the complications rise. For example, beginning in the late 1990s, a burgeoning business arose for US companies in providing Internet Service Providers overseas with a satellite-based connection to the US Internet backbone. The business grew like crazy, because the vast majority of Internet connectivity and content was in the US, and most developing nations have lousy and expensive international telephone service. But there was a major challenge to the business: how to collect what you're owed by ISPs in Bangladesh and Nigeria, Brazil and Peru. Collection problems drove a number of the new entrepreneurial companies out of business.

The point of this discussion is to remind you to always, always take the credit issue into consideration before you write the proposal, or at least before you close the deal. You may be able to reassure yourself with a few minutes of thought. You may choose to use credit reporting services to dig deeper. You may have to ask for credit references or, in the case of overseas companies, to consult with the US Department of Commerce, or to demand a letter of credit. Extending credit is always a judgment call, but it should at least be made with your eyes wide open.

What to Put in Your Proposal

Thinking about skipping this section, because you already know what to put in a proposal? Don't. We'll bet you a mail-order steak that there's at least one missing ingredient in your current proposals, and that adding it will significantly increase your success rate.

Here are the basic components of an effective B2B proposal:

- **Purpose** – In a few short paragraphs, clearly define the situation that has led to this proposal, and the business problem that it seeks to solve.

- **Scope or Solution** – Describe how you will solve the Suspect's problem using your company's products or services, with enough detail about your processes, systems and facilities to make clear how it addresses the business problem.

- **Timeline** – Provide the Suspect with a general or specific schedule for implementing the solution. Because such things typically depend on the customer's schedule, we like to provide a Gant chart format and include a caveat that adherence to the schedule depends on the customer's ability to respond in a timely fashion.

Action	W1	W2	W3	W4	W5
Step 1	▓				
Step 2		▓	▓		
Step 3				▓	▓
W= week					

- **Value** – Explain in the same terms uncovered by your implication and solution questions the value to the Suspect of solving that business problem. This establishes the context in which you want your solution and its cost to be evaluated.

- **Price** – Finally, it's time to reveal what this will all cost the Suspect, expressed in easily-understood terms.

- **Next Steps** – Explain clearly what will happen next: that you will follow up and, if terms are acceptable, execute an agreement.

Do We Owe You a Steak?

The one thing that most B2B companies leave out of their proposal is the clear and persuasive explanation of value. It's not surprising. We're all eager to explain our wonderful solution to the Suspect's problem, and to write glowing paragraphs about our processes, systems and facilities. Then we're stunned when the Suspect tells us that it costs too much.

If you've done all that good work during the Appointment to tease out the implications of the buyer's problem and position your product or service as the solution — for God's sake make sure that this information goes into your proposal. And include it before the price is finally revealed, so that when the Suspect gets to the price tag, the cost is evaluated in comparison with the value you promise to deliver.

So, do we owe you that steak? If so, send an email to lzacharilla@alananthony.com. Include a recent proposal with your value statement, and your meat-by-mail will be on its way in a matter of days.

Submitting the Proposal

There are many ways to submit a proposal, depending on how much money is involved and how much effort went into developing the proposal.

Multi-million-dollar proposals typically involve a lot of time and expense on the part of the vendor. Some of the big IT outsourcing companies estimate that they invest $100,000 worth of time and expense in each major proposal, because they have to learn so much about the Suspect's current operations and requirements. At the other end of the spectrum are proposals for the sale of individual pieces of equipment or small systems, small service projects and the like. These are mostly boilerplate based on past sales or projects. In either case, you schedule a meeting (or phone call, if necessary) with your Inside Coach to review it, and then present the proposal at the meeting. In practice, it's not always possible to get that meeting, due to either the prospect's schedule or your own, and you must sometimes submit the proposal and then follow up. This is never the best approach, but it's better than not submitting a proposal at all.

For complex solutions, it can often help to submit a "concept proposal." This defines the problem to be solved, explains the value of the solution, and lays out the scope. No timeline or price is mentioned. The goal is to confirm your understanding in more detail than was possible in the sales meeting, and to start the buy-in process for the Suspect. When you follow up, you will gain feedback that makes your final proposal more persuasive.

For a large deal, the ideal approach is to have your Inside Coach arrange a presentation at which you can get face time with senior decision-makers and sell the value of your solution. Of course, in most cases, you won't get to do things this way. You'll have to submit a proposal by a deadline. It will be evaluated by a faceless committee, and you will have no other opportunity to influence the outcome. But it never hurts to ask for the sale to go the way you want it to go.

Setting the Stopwatch

Once that proposal is submitted, your follow-up effort has two goals: to establish that the price quoted is not, by itself, a reason for rejection; and to set a deadline for the decision with the Suspect. The first indicator is largely negative — if the Suspect doesn't object categorically to the price, you're in. The second indicator is not hard and fast. The deadline may be soft (2-3 weeks) or it may move back ("we can't move on this until after the end of the quarter"), but the existence of a deadline focuses the Suspect and gives you an indication of the priority the Suspect places on it.

Suspect? Did we say "Suspect?" By now, with an un-rejected proposal in hand and a deadline for decision, this company has become a Prospect. They are the closest thing to money in the bank except...well, money in the bank.

CHAPTER 17

To Close or Not to Close

In the introduction to this book, we said that the biggest mistake people make in marketing and sales is to focus all their attention on the close. Why? Because selling is a cumulative process. If you have done everything right up to this point, the sale is ready to close, unless unforeseen factors get in the way. You can still pooch it by failing to ask for the sale, creating complications or slacking off when you need to stay focused. But the close of the sale is the result of a long series of actions, decision and accidents that have either developed the opportunity or caused it to wither away.

In his book *The Art of War*, written some 2,500 years ago, the Chinese general Sun Tzu put it like this: "To fight and conquer in all your battles is not supreme excellence; supreme excellence consists in breaking the enemy's resistance without fighting." In other words, most battles are won or lost before the armies take to the field. The same is true of the close.

The Four Fates

Once submitted, your quote or proposal is undergoing one of four fates.

It is being seriously considered by the decision-maker(s), usually in competition with other proposals.

It is being sidetracked by unexpected crises or opportunities, and your contacts must turn their attention elsewhere for a period of time.

It is falling victim to a change in priority at the company, often due to financial reverses or the hiring of a new top executive team. Your contacts are keeping their heads down, polishing up their resumes or are already out on the street.

Despite all appearances, the Prospect was just kicking the tires, possibly to check up on its current vendor, and there was never a real opportunity there.

Obviously, you are following up on a schedule agreed to by the Prospect. You are looking for feedback on the proposal, particularly for an opportunity to sharpen the definition of requirements, revise specifications and generally engage in making the solution a perfect fit for the Prospect's needs.

There are two key indicators of success: response and time.

- Does the Prospect respond to your follow-up? The best case is that your calls or emails are returned promptly, and that the response gives you useful information. The worst case is that the Prospect suddenly does a "mole" and disappears underground. Your calls and emails go unreturned, or are returned weeks late with no useful information.

- Having a set a deadline for the decision, does the Prospect keep to it? If there are delays, are they reasonable and limited, or does the deadline keep slipping, becoming vaguer with each delay?

This is the agonizing time for people who sell. You are so near to the close, but you haven't been able to make the Prospect step over the magic line. You need patience and (at least the illusion of) serenity. Above all, you need to act like you don't need the sale, because any hint of desperation in your voice or manner will raise doubts in the Prospect's mind. The more you can think of this sale as just another game in a long season, the more successful you will tend to be.

What to Do If You Lose

Few of us need counsel on handling success. If you get the sale, you can pump your fist in the air or take your Significant Other out to dinner. You can make sure the hand-off from sales to customer service or operations goes smoothly. And you can schedule yourself to connect with the new Customer at the right times to ensure renewal of the contract.

But what do you do if you lose? Believe it or not, this is probably more important to your long-term success than how you handle winning. Because we always learn more from our failures than we do from successes.

If you don't get the sale, the best thing you can do is to talk to the Prospect. It's also one of the hardest things you can do, emotionally speaking. And you may also have a tough time actually contacting the Prospect, because he or she will assume that you are trying to revive the sale and may genuinely feel guilty to boot. So your phone and email messages, and your actual conversation with the Prospect, have to make it clear that you are calmly seeking information, not making a last-ditch effort to overturn the decision. What choice was made? How was the decision reached? What were the factors that favored a competitor? Is there something you personally could have done differently?

The answers to these questions are of immense value. They may signal the need to improve your company's products or services. They may suggest a new marketing strategy. And they might help you to do something new, or stop doing something old, that can improve your success rate in the future.

CHAPTER 18

The Formula for Success

Chapters 12-17 have been about the art and science of selling. We hope they have offered useful advice to the person who goes out into the field to create new revenues.

Our final chapters are for people who have to manage that process. But whether you sell, manage or have to do both, they will help you do it more effectively and correct problems before they become serious. Which means that you and your team succeed more often.

What Must I Do Today
To Meet My Goals Tomorrow?

In Chapter 13, we defined the stages of the typical B2B sale. Now we're going to put those stages into a framework that makes it possible to manage the long-cycle, high-value B2B selling process, and to know exactly what you need to do today in order to accomplish your sales goals tomorrow.

We call it The Formula for Success, and we must credit a colleague and Practice Leader, Robert Rogus, for this particular formulation of a classic approach to sales management.

In Chapter 13, we presented a chart that showed the sale progressing in stages from Contact to Suspect, Prospect to Customer. On the next page, we show another version of that chart with some new information.

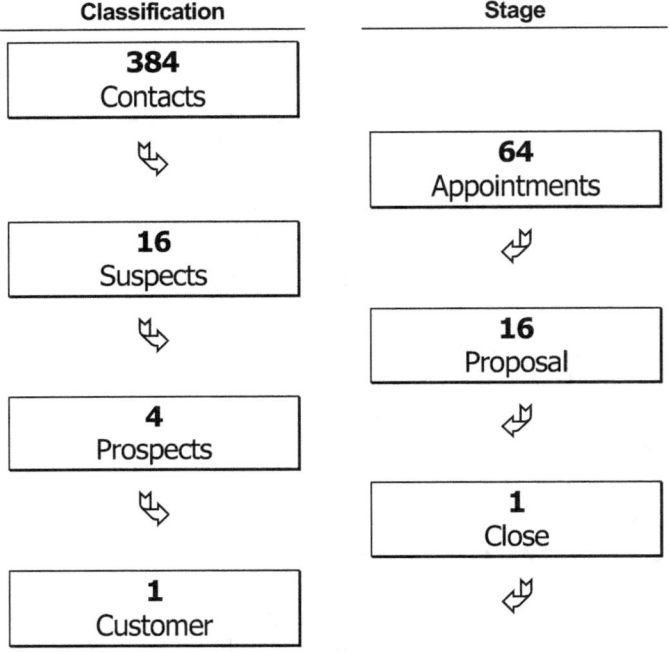

Classification	Stage
384 Contacts	
	64 Appointments
16 Suspects	
	16 Proposal
4 Prospects	
	1 Close
1 Customer	

This chart illustrates the fact that you've got to kiss a lot of frogs to find a prince. On average, you need to reach out to 6 Contacts to get 1 Appointment, have 4 Appointments to find 1 Suspect, submit 4 Proposals to Suspects to find 1 Prospect, and chase 4 Prospects to close 1 Customer. Following this logic to its conclusion, you have to reach out to 384 Contacts over a period of time to, on average, close 1 Customer.

These are averages, and individual performance can vary widely. Some people are great canvassers and need only 4 Contacts to get an Appointment. When you're on a winning streak, you might be able to close 1 out every 2 Prospects. But these averages are a useful guide until you know your own performance, or those of your people, on an individual basis.

Reaching Your Goal

You can use these averages, or your individual performance numbers, to figure out exactly what you or your employees need to do to reach your goals. To do this, you need two numbers.

The dollar value of the average sale. If your company produced $5 million last year from 50 customers, the value of the average sale was $100,000. If you company produced $90 million in revenue last year from 200 customers, the average sale was worth $450,000. (Actually, this calculation isn't exact, because there are probably multiple sales to some customers. But it's close enough.)

The sales cycle of your business. How long does it take, on average, to close a sale? Some sales happen almost overnight. Others stretch on and on until you give up hope — and then suddenly close. But for every business, there's an average between the fast and the slow that is the sales cycle of the company.

We've asked dozens and dozens of B2B salespeople how long it took to close the average sale, and the unvarying answer is: "Well, it depends." That's right, it depends. But there's a simple reason that most salespeople can't tell you their sales cycle. To figure it out requires you to keep track of the time it takes to close a sample group of sales. And who wants to do that? Sales is all about performance, and you don't have time to screw around with collecting useless information. But this is information you definitely need to know. And here's how you obtain it.

First, make a guess about your average sales cycle, based on the intuition gained from experience. Use this until you have better data. It won't be perfect, but it will be a lot better than nothing.

Second, every time you have an Appointment, note the date and the company name in a notebook or computer file. If you're good about record-keeping for meetings, you may already have this information. If not, start today and continue for three months. Then, six months later — nine months from now — go back and see which of them have become Customers. Count the days, weeks or months elapsed for each one and average the durations.

If there seem to be too few customers in this group to represent your average success rate, then your sales cycle is longer than six months. That's useful information right there, particularly if you have been working on the assumption that it's shorter. But it means you have to come back in another three months, and possibly another three months after that, to look at the data again. Sure, it's a pain. But it allows you to *know* how long, on average, it takes from "Hello, my name is…" to the signature and handshake. And in this case, knowledge is power.

Get Cracking

Let's say your goal for new sales this year is $1 million in new sales. What do you have to do to make your goal?

Here's where the first number comes in. If the average value of a sale at your company is $100,000, you need to close 10 sales to make your goal. If the average value is $250,000, you need four sales to meet your quota.

And if you need four sales, that's an average of one per quarter. Fail to sell anything for six months, and you've got to do two per quarter. Leave it too long, and you've got to get them all in 90 days.

Here's where the second number comes in. Let's say your sales cycle is 90 days. That is, the Appointment you have on April Fool's Day has a reasonable chance of producing a Customer by the Fourth of July. Applying the Formula from page 134, you find that you have to reach out to 384 Contacts every quarter in order to close that Customer. That's six new Contacts a day. That's a lot of research, qualification, telephone calls and emails.

But the Contacts are only the beginning. Using those Contacts, you need to have 64 Appointments, or an average of one a day. Based on those one-a-day meetings, you need to issue 16 Proposals, or a bit more than five proposals per month. And so on and so forth.

In other words, it's a numbers game. The bad news is, you'd better get cracking. The good news is that you can make the numbers work for you.

CHAPTER 19

Tracking the Sale

How does the Formula for Success make the numbers work
for you? It's like any other good management system. It helps
you to set priorities week-by-week and acts as an early warning system for trouble ahead.

Setting Priorities

In the example at the end of the last chapter, we saw that
achieving your goal was going to take the following kind of
performance:

	Weekly	Monthly	Quarterly
Appointments with Contacts	5	22	64
Proposals to Suspects		6	16
Prospects		+1	4
Customers			1

Laying it out this way lets you see immediately where you're
doing well and where you need to focus more effort. If you
issued 8 new Proposals last month, that's great. You're ahead
of the curve. But if you only managed 10 Appointments,
there's trouble ahead. Those 10 Appointments will probably
allow you to issue no more three Proposals and, if you're
lucky, identify one Prospect. Not enough to land the Customer
you need.

Tracking the Sale

Have you already figured out where we're going with this? That's right: we're going to ask you to collect more "useless" information.

We assume that, if you've read this far, you have already started rating every company in your database or card file or notebook as a Contact, Suspect or Prospect. And that you're updating this ranking every time you connect with that company; that is, after a good Appointment, you're changing the ranking from Contact to Suspect.

The next step is to keep a log of key sales activity in order to feed your understanding of your own performance. In other words, whether you are selling or are managing sales, you need a *sales tracking system*.

Here's the information that your system needs to capture.

- Number of Appointments, whether face-to-face or telecom-based sales calls
- Number of Proposals issued
- Number of new Prospects

The best way to manage this information is in the form of a weekly sales activity report, due on Monday and covering the preceding week. Here's what should appear in a typical report:

No. Appointments:	5
No. Proposals:	2
No. New Prospects:	1

In addition to the sales activity report, you should also maintain a sales forecast, which is basically a list of Prospects, updated weekly, that includes the company names, the product(s) or service(s) being considered, the estimated value of the sale, the date the proposal was submitted and the estimated probability of closing, based on the salesperson's follow-up. It might look like this:

- 140 -

Prospect	Prod/Serv	Value	Prop Date	Prob.
XYX Company	MasterWidget	$85,000	3/11/03	80%
Complexeon	MiniWidget-X	$120,000	3/25/03	50%

With these two simple documents — a weekly sales activity report and an up-to-date sales forecast — you have all the tools you need. You can do this on paper, on a computer spreadsheet, with a complex database or any other way that works best for you and your organization. The technology doesn't matter; what matters is doing it week by week, month after month.

The Payoff from Reporting

All of this pain-in-the-neck reporting pays off for you, individually and as a part of a team, in three ways.

First and most important, the weekly activity reports create a cumulative picture of how well you are performing against your goals. You can add up the numbers from four reports to see how you are doing on a monthly basis, compared with how many Appointments, Proposals and Closes you need to meet your goals. The point is not to give yourself or your salespeople ulcers. The point is to be able to make course corrections long before your quarter-end, year-end or whatever the deadline may be.

For example, if the number of Appointments is running consistently short of what's needed, then the solution is to devote more time to prospecting among Contacts, or to work on prospecting skills in order to get more Appointments from the same number of Contacts. On the other hand, if the number of Appointments is high but the number of Proposals is low, it suggests that time and effort needs to be applied to making Appointments more productive. (See Chapters 14 and 15.)

All of us bring to the selling process a different mix of talents. For that reason, we experience a different level of challenge in the various stages of the sale. We've never met anybody who really loves prospecting, but some find it easy and productive. Others excel at qualifying during the Appointment. As a result, they issue fewer Proposals, but each one has a much higher probability of leading to a sale. Wherever your strengths are, they will be accompanied by weaknesses. Examining your weekly activity will show you where the weaknesses are, and create the opportunity to improve. You can coach your salespeople, go on Appointments with them and offer feedback, or whatever else comes to mind. Then you can see, in black-and-white, if the remedial action changes the weekly performance.

Custom Fit

Second, the activity reports allow you to customize the Formula in order to better predict the personal performance of each salesperson. Because we have different strengths and weaknesses, the Formula as outlined on page 134 will not apply to everyone. Your talent for prospecting may mean that you only need four cold calls, on average, to get an Appointment. But you may need more than four Appointments in order to find a real Suspect. Examining the activity reports will let you create a personal Formula for each person who sells, which will improve sales predictability.

Third, the sales forecast gives you a different, forward-looking view of performance against the goal, one based on total sales rather than activity. That's valuable in itself. It also allows the person responsible for sales to keep management informed at all times, whether the news is good or bad. In business, there are successes and there are failures, and then there are surprises. In our experience, it is the surprises that get you into the deepest trouble.

CHAPTER 20

Compensating Success

Salespeople are unique among the employees of most B2B companies in that most of their compensation is directly tied to measures of their success. This is partly a matter of convenience: there are few other jobs where it is so easy to measure success. It is also a testament to the vital function of sales in the life of the business. Like oxygen for the body, it is something no company can live without.

Basics of Sales Compensation

There are as many approaches to compensating salespeople as there are sure-fire betting systems at the racetrack. But most share a few common characteristics that should form the basis of your own compensation system:

1. A base salary that is deliberately inadequate to live on, so that the incentive portion of total compensation is a necessity rather than a luxury.

2. A commission on:
    A. Sales to new customers or on sales of additional products or services to existing customers.
    B. Re-signing contracts with existing customers, which is usually lower than the commission on new sales.

The commission structure depends on the nature of what you're selling, and on the current priorities of the business. For businesses that sell products, the structure can be simple.

If you sell MaxiWidgets to a new customer, then Commission A applies on the value of that particular sale. If you sell more MaxiWidgets to that customer, then Commission B applies to the sales value. If you sell DigiStuff to the same customer, then Commission A applies.

ILLUSTRATION 19-1

Sale	Comp. Level	Percentage
MaxiWidgets to a new customer	A	3%
More MaxiWidgets to the same customer	B	2%
DigiStuff to the same customer	A	3%

Most businesses that sell services, which typically have recurring revenues, make some variations on this theme. If you sell SuperService to a new customer, then Commission A applies — but to what sales value? A typical structure is to apply one commission level (say 3%) to the first 12 months of revenues, a lower commission (say 2%) to the second 12 months, and an even lower commission (say 1%) to revenues starting with the third 12 months through the life of the contract. This reflects the reduced involvement of the salesperson with that account over time.

ILLUSTRATION 19-2

Sale	Comp. Level	Percentage		
		Yr 1	Yr 2	Yr 3
SuperService to a new customer	A	3%	2%	1%
Renewing customer to SuperService	B	2%	1%	1%
MaxiService to the same customer	A	3%	2%	1%

Re-signing the same customer to a new contract invokes Commission B, which may jump the salesperson's competition to 2% for a year, and then step it back down to the lowest level.

The Point of the Compensation Structure

The point of all sales compensation systems is to set priorities for the salespeople and to reward them for achievements that are in line with those priorities. The recurring-revenue structure described above makes selling new customers (or new services to existing customers) the top priority. But salespeople are also rewarded for paying attention to continuing customer satisfaction, and for successfully maintaining the relationship through renewal of the contract. However, a salesperson who is stronger at maintaining relationships than at hunting new customers is not going to prosper under this system. And that may be exactly what you want.

It is possible to motivate almost any selling behavior by setting the appropriate commission. While this structure rewards the hunt for new customers, it is also possible to emphasize contract renewals by setting the commission for these at a high level. This would be appropriate for a recurring-revenue business that is having trouble keeping customers and wants its salespeople to focus on this as renewal time approaches. Of course, if customer dissatisfaction is caused by operational or financial problems beyond the control of the sales department, jiggering commissions will do little to solve it.

Whatever system you are using, you will need to change it from time to time. The priorities of the business will inevitably change, and only by revising the compensation system can you truly refocus the attention of salespeople. We all like money, but people who go into sales find it a more powerful incentive than most, and good ones will immediately point their energies to where the money is.

Changing people's compensation, of course, must be done with care. Be sure to give your salespeople plenty of warning of the change and clear reasons for it. Never make the mistake of applying it retroactively to past contracts, as this changes the rules in mid-game and can create a great deal of bitterness.

Territories

As soon as you have more than one person selling for you, you need territories. Sales territories define where a salesperson may hunt for business and receive full commission for the resulting sale. Dividing the market into territories avoids confusion for your potential customers from being approached by more than one representative of your company. It also keeps your employees from competing with each other to win the same piece of business, and fighting over the commission from a successful sale.

Territories may be geographic and defined by anything from uptown and downtown to zip codes, area codes or state borders. Territories can also be by industrial category within the same geographic area. This is particularly useful for companies that believe they can best serve customers by taking a vertical-industry approach.

The single most important thing to keep in mind when devising territories and assigning people to them is fairness. Ideally, each territory should present salespeople with an equal opportunity for success. This means avoiding territories which contain unequal numbers of potential customers, or having some territories with mostly large companies and others with mostly small companies. Since you will never have a comprehensive list of all the companies that might buy from you, devising territories always involves subjective judgment. You do the best you can based on experience, and adjust as necessary based on results.

The New Salesperson

When a new salesperson joins your team, you cannot expect instant performance at a high level, unless you were able to hire a "rainmaker" who comes with a Rolodex full of industry contacts. The sales compensation system must, therefore, avoid penalizing the new hire for taking the time to learn the business, become acquainted with the territory and get to know the customers.

One common approach is to provide a base salary plus a "draw" against future commissions. This effectively guarantees the employee's income during a pre-determined period of time, from six to nine months in most cases. In our experience, however, it is a better idea to simply offer a higher base salary that, at stated future dates, will ratchet downward in steps to the average. The problem with the draw is that you are paying the salesperson in advance for future sales. So when he or she makes some of those sales, they see no change in their compensation, which is deflating for people who are used to instant rewards. The higher base salary will cost you somewhat more in the first year if the salesperson is successful. But if he or she *is* successful, do you really care? With a new hire who doesn't work out, the cost is the same as with a "draw" system.

How Much?

If you are implementing your first commission system, or reworking one you inherited, how do you go about it?

Start with a dollar figure that represents the desired compensation for a successful salesperson. What should you pay an employee who achieves your goals, based on what's competitive in your industry and geographic area? You may already know this from experience in the industry. If not, this information is often available from industry associations, trade magazines, or research services.

Once you have a target figure, you divide it into two portions: a base salary and commission. The base salary should be 40-60% of the total, depending on how much pressure you are comfortable putting on your sales reps.

To set the commissions, assign sales quotas to that employee for new sales and resales. Then figure out how much commission you need to pay on those sales to produce the necessary total compensation. You usually have to have to calculate it back and forth several times, using different assumptions about sales quotas and commissions, before you find something workable.

Gaming the System

No matter what compensation system you have in place, be sure of one thing. Some of your salespeople will eventually figure out how to "game" it so that they get paid even when they don't produce what you want. After all, you work on the compensation system once and then have to turn your attention to other issues. They live with it week in and week out. So naturally, they come to understand it better than you do. This is one reason why you must plan to change your system from time to time, even if your company's priorities do not shift. It's the only way to ensure that the system is reasonably fair to all — the highly ethical and the gamesters — while also accomplishing your company's goals.

So, Why Aren't Your People Selling More?

We hope that the time you spent with this book has provided some answers to this critical question. The answers may be strategic. They may involve marketing tactics or the fundamentals of organizing and managing a sales effort. Or perhaps it's a combination of all three.

We began our discussion with strategy, and did it for a simple reason. Before you start trying to improve *how* you do things, it's a good idea to make sure you are doing something that makes sense. But there are also dangers to getting bogged down in a deep strategic review — one that may result in your tackling new markets or changing your mix of products and services — until you are confident of your basic marketing and sales tactics. If you can't hit singles and doubles, your strategy for winning the World Series isn't likely to pay off.

So it's helpful to start by thinking through and documenting the basics of your strategy: who you are selling to, what you are selling, and so forth. But before taking it further, you need to make sure that the marketing and sales machine is hitting on all cylinders.

Start with sales, because the effort you invest there will have the quickest payoff. See if you have the basics in place. Do you categorize potential buyers in a meaningful way? Do you track sales well enough to help yourself or your salespeople to improve their performance? Can you predict results over the long term with some degree of reliability?

Once you have an effective sales management system in place, turn your attention to marketing. Are you adequately supporting your salespeople? What marketing tactics are you missing that might be effective? Once you identify some tactics you would like to try, introduce them one at a time, in a structured way, and see if each one produces results.

When you know that marketing and sales are doing what they should, you will profit immensely by conducting an in-depth review of your strategy. Are there opportunities in new markets that your company is missing? Can you change the way you package your services or products to open up new doors? Can you partner with another company to cross-sell to each other's customers?

Seeing the opportunity is one thing. Seizing it is another. That's why you need a powerful marketing and sales operation in place, so that you can bring the innovation to market in a reasonable time and give it the best chance of success.

As Peter Drucker said in the quote that opened this book, when you drill down to the basics of your business, marketing and innovation are all you'll find. They are the irreducible forces that will drive your business to succeed, or drive it under. Everything else is just...well, BS.

Good luck!

Have a comment, complaint or suggestion about this book?
Send us an email at lzacharilla@alananthony.com or call us at +1 212-825-1582 extension 12, and we'll gladly respond.

Robert Bell and Louis Zacharilla are senior partners of Alan/Anthony, Inc. (www.alananthony.com), a partnership that specializes in working with B2B companies that face serious challenges in customer creation.

Robert Bell has nearly 20 years of experience as a consultant for both profit-driven and non-profit organizations operating in the IT outsourcing, telecommunications, and financial services industries. He is also a frequent speaker at telecommunications industry conferences and the author of articles in *The Municipal Journal of Telecommunications Policy, Telecommunications, Asian Communications, Phone+ International* and *INFORM*. He has appeared on segments of ABC World News and the Discovery Channel.

After a career in advertising, where his work included the award-winning "Be All You Can Be" campaign for the US Army, Louis Zacharilla began consulting in 1983 with B2B companies in telecommunications, real estate and industrial applications on public relations, brand, and business development issues. A popular speaker at conferences and award programs, he has written for publications including *Continental*, the in-flight magazine, *New York Real Estate Journal, Real Estate Weekly, Document Processing Technology, Enterprise Systems Journal* and *Information Executive*. He is also an adjunct professor at Fordham University in New York, where he teaches a course on marketing and the media.

In addition to consulting, the partners also manage two nonprofit trade associations in the satellite industry: the World Teleport Association (www.worldteleport.org) and the Society of Satellite Professionals International (www.sspi.org).

www.ingramcontent.com/pod-product-compliance
Lightning Source LLC
Chambersburg PA
CBHW060748180626
46818CB00002B/506